'Do you think tl you to Napier?'

'I hope not. I don't v ————— ——————
ever.' The last word was spat with vehemence.

Ryan regarded her with concern. 'In that case you'll have to take care you're not caught on the rebound,' he warned. 'If a handsome stranger comes along and is particularly nice to you—you might fall flat at his feet. Metaphorically speaking, of course,' he added with a twinkle in his eye.

'That's most unlikely,' she retorted coldly. 'Just as you appear to be allergic to women, I'm in a similar frame of mind concerning men. At the moment I look upon them as being anything but trustworthy.'

'Thank you very much,' he growled. 'Not even present company excepted, I notice.'

Judy decided to be frank. 'I just feared you might be referring to yourself as the handsome stranger,' she said, while giving a light laugh to soften her words.

Miriam Macgregor has written eight books of historical non-fiction, but turned to romance in 1980. Many years on a sheep and cattle farm in New Zealand gave her an insight to rural life. She lived on the coast at Westshore, a suburb of Napier, where her desk overlooked Hawke Bay, a corner of the South Pacific Ocean. She has recently swapped the Pacific Ocean for the Atlantic and emigrated to Middlesex, England. She enjoys painting in oils, water colours and pastels, and does her own housework and gardening while planning her romantic novels.

A MOST DETERMINED BACHELOR

BY
MIRIAM MACGREGOR

First published in Great Britain 1999
Harlequin Mills & Boon Limited,
Eton House, 18-24 Paradise Road, Richmond, Surrey TW9 1SR

© Miriam Macgregor 1999

ISBN 0 263 81505 6

Set in Times Roman 10 on 11 pt.
02-9903 59291 C1

Printed and bound in Norway
by AIT Trondheim AS, Trondheim

CHAPTER ONE

THE small boy tugged at Judy's sleeve. 'Isn't Uncle Ryan here to meet us?' he queried anxiously.

Judith Arledge's blue eyes scanned the crowd in the small New Zealand airport. A buzz of happy chatter vibrated on the air as people greeted friends or relatives who had recently disembarked from the plane that had just touched down at Napier. It was nice to be welcomed with enthusiasm, she thought wistfully, then wondered about the man who was supposed to be meeting herself and Robin.

Where was Ryan Ellison?

'We'd better sit down and wait,' she said with a hint of resignation, then took Robin's hand and led him towards two empty seats.

'Where is Uncle Ryan?' the boy demanded fretfully.

Judy gave what she hoped was a reassuring smile. 'Perhaps he's been held up. No doubt he'll be along soon.' This, she hoped, would prove to be a fact, otherwise she didn't know what to do or where to go.

Searching in her mind for comfort, she recalled the words of Robin's grandmother. 'Ryan will definitely be there to meet you,' Hilda Simmons had promised, when making arrangements with Judy to take the little boy from Christchurch, in the South Island, to Napier, in the North Island.

'But—how shall I recognise him?' Judy had queried doubtfully. She was not at all happy with the task that had been presented to her, and not for the first time wondered how she'd been catapulted into accepting it. But at least it would give her a short period away from Christchurch, which was something she felt herself to be in dire need of.

5

Hilda Simmons had been anything but vague. A faint snort had escaped her as she'd said, 'Don't worry, you'll spot him at once. Ryan Ellison will stride into that airport as though he owns the place. Every woman will turn to look at him. I can tell you he's a man who stands out in a crowd. I suppose it's his success that gives him such an air of confidence.'

'But—what does he *look* like?' Judy had persisted.

'Tall—broad-shouldered—dark auburn hair. But you needn't be concerned about him recognising *you*.' The older woman had cast a dismissive glance over Judy's blonde wavy hair. 'It's *Robin* he'll be searching for. My Verna's *son*—you understand?'

Robin's voice interrupted her thoughts. 'Judy—is Uncle Ryan my *real* uncle, or just a pretend uncle like Uncle Alan?'

Judy shifted uneasily in her seat. 'You can forget Uncle Alan,' she told him firmly. 'You'll not be seeing *him* again.'

'Why?' Hazel eyes regarded her with surprise.

'Because I'll not be seeing him again, either,' she said through compressed lips.

'Why?' The boy's eyes widened.

She tried to remain calm. 'Because he's not to be trusted, so please don't mention his name again—*ever*. As for Uncle Ryan—I'm not sure where he fits in.' She realised the boy knew little about his relatives, and that for some reason his mother and grandmother forced him to lead a sheltered life. It made her speak guardedly while turning to brush back his fringe of dark brown hair, that held hints of red when the sun shone on it. 'It's possible that Uncle is just a courtesy title,' she added.

'What's courtesy?'

'It means being polite,' she explained patiently. Then, regarding the freckles sprinkled across his nose and cheeks, she went on, 'As you are only six, and he's a mature man, it's more polite for you to call him Uncle.'

'Are you mature, Judy?'

She smiled ruefully. 'At twenty-three I should be, although I'm now beginning to wonder about it.' How could a mature person be taken in by a man as disloyal as Alan Draper? she pondered. She should have seen through him from the beginning.

Robin swept away her bitter thoughts. 'Shall I be going to school in Napier?'

'No, dear. It's July. The schools are still closed for the winter holidays. Your grandmother says you've been rather bronchial lately, and as Napier is a warmer place than Christchurch she thought it would be wise to get you away from the cold South Island winds. That's why she rang Uncle Ryan about spending some time with him.'

'What's bronchial?'

She simplified the answer. 'Chest colds that make you cough a lot. Have you been like that?'

He shook his head.

Judy frowned, her blue eyes regarding the boy thoughtfully. She saw quite a lot of Robin. Almost every day after school he came through a hole in the hedge dividing his grandmother's and her parents' properties, but so far she'd noticed nothing bronchial about him. He appeared to be a perfectly healthy lad who wolfed down the cookies and orange drinks she often provided for him. In fact it was this kindness to the lad that had landed her in her present situation.

Sitting at the kitchen table one day, Robin had said casually, 'My Gran is *very*, *very* cross. She's so *angry* she's nearly crying.'

Judy had looked at him in amazement. She could imagine Hilda Simmons being cross, because it was a state not at all foreign to her. But for her neighbour to reach the stage of tears was something she was unable to visualise. Should she go next door to see if there was anything she could do to help? Judy was the type of person who liked to help.

At the same time she hesitated, fearing that Hilda Simmons might consider she was intruding upon a private matter. Nevertheless, the thought of her being so upset disturbed Judy, particularly as she was an elderly widow whose daughter, Robin's mother, was away at present. Tentatively, she asked, 'Why is your gran so upset?'

His mouth half full, Robin said, ''Cos Mrs Fulton won't do something she wants her to do.'

Judy looked at him thoughtfully. 'Could I help? Is it something I could do for her?'

'I don't know…'

Judy made a decision. She might be putting herself in the position of being told to mind her own business, but if her neighbour needed assistance she felt it should be offered. Impulsively, she said, 'Finish your drink and we'll go and see your gran.'

Robin had not exaggerated the extent of his grandmother's anger. She was frothing mad, yet her face cleared and a speculative look crept into her eyes as Judy stepped into the neighbouring kitchen.

'Robin said you need a little help,' the latter began.

'Oh, I do—*I do!*' Hilda Simmons exclaimed. She was a tall, dominant woman of generous proportions, and her dark eyes held a piercing glint. People usually found themselves doing as she demanded, but in this case she did not appear to have been completely successful. 'That wretched Fulton woman has let me down,' she went on in an aggrieved tone. 'She's one of my bridge players. She was going to Napier and had promised to take Robin with her. She was to leave him with Ryan—but now she's had to cancel her trip.'

Who was Ryan? Judy wondered at that stage.

Hilda's wrath then turned towards her daughter. 'It was very selfish of Verna to go skiing at the beginning of the school holidays,' she complained. 'She has no right to put the responsibility for Robin on me. She *knows* he's becoming more than I can cope with. She *knows* I can't allow my

good works to suffer because of a small boy who is often
very naughty.'

The last words were accompanied by a dark glare towards Robin, who stood listening with a sullen look on his
small face and his lower lip thrust slightly forward.

'It would be *dreadful* if he had one of his tantrums in
front of my bridge ladies,' Hilda added, the mere thought
causing a hint of horror to creep into her voice.

Judy made no reply. She considered Hilda Simmons to
be an overbearing woman who was capable of coping with
anything. Nor did she find it difficult to imagine her placing
the responsibility of Robin on somebody else herself. As
for the 'good works'—they were little more than afternoon
bridge parties which resulted in a few dollars going to char-
ity. Even so, Hilda's next words had given her a shock.

Taking a deep breath, the older woman drew herself to
her full height as she said, 'Well—you asked if there was
anything you could do to help. As it happens, there is. You
can take Robin to Napier and leave him with Ryan Ellison.'

'*Me—?*' The word came out like a squeak as Judy gaped
at her.

'Of course you'll be paid. That should be a help, considering you're currently out of work.' Hilda paused before
adding thoughtfully, 'I feel sure he'll be safe with Ryan.'

Her last words surprised Judy. '*Safe? Safe from what?*'

Hilda ignored the question as she said, 'Don't allow him
to talk to any strange men. One hears so much about these
ghastly people…'

The thought made Judy shudder, but she managed to
speak calmly. 'I think you're worrying needlessly, Mrs
Simmons. Air hostesses will do the job for you. Children
often travel in the care of hostesses. They're very reliable—'

Hilda pursed thin lips. 'But they'd be strangers to Robin,
whereas he *knows* you,' she said, with unexpected grand-
motherly concern. 'I'm afraid he's not very good with

women he doesn't know, although he's quite at ease with men.'

A sigh escaped Judy. 'Very well, I'll take him. Job-hunting will have to wait until I return to Christchurch.'

Hilda breathed a sigh of relief. 'Thank you, my dear. And don't forget to warn Ryan about what happens if the boy becomes unduly upset. You *know* what I mean…'

Judy had nodded without uttering the dreaded word *bed-wetting*.

Hilda stood looking at Judy reflectively, her dark eyes taking in the latter's lovely face, with its clear complexion, straight nose and sweetly generous mouth. The blonde hair curling about the slim shoulders made her look much younger than her twenty-three years, and, almost as if noticing her neighbour's beauty for the first time, the older woman spoke firmly. 'Of course there'll be no need for you to stay in Napier. Ryan's housekeeper will take care of Robin as soon as he becomes accustomed to her. You may come home the next day.'

Judy felt puzzled. 'I can? But—who will bring Robin home?'

'Naturally, Verna will make the trip to fetch him. It's high time she made contact with Ryan again. Actually—he should have married her *years* ago.' Hilda's eyes blazed with a flash of anger. 'But has he done so? No—*he has not*. According to his housekeeper, he's thrown himself into agricultural pursuits and has become a veritable land baron. She said it's difficult to know whether he owns the land, or whether the land owns him. She also said his house sees as much social life as a hermit's cave. But of course Verna would alter all that.'

Robin broke into Judy's ponderings, his voice holding an anxious note as he said, 'I don't think Uncle Ryan is pleased we're coming to stay with him. That's why he's not here to meet us.'

Judy sent him a curious glance, but forced herself to speak casually. 'Why do you say that?'

''Cos Gran kept frowning when she talked to him on the phone. She was very, very cross. I think Uncle Ryan was cross too.' His eyes looked at her pleadingly. 'Judy—could we go home—*now*?'

She felt disturbed. 'No, dear, I'm afraid that's impossible. At least, not today.' Had a word of welcome been missing from the other end of the line? she wondered. Her arm went about Robin in a comforting gesture as she added, 'If Uncle Ryan stays cross with us we shall go home very soon,' she promised.

By this time the airport was emptying. Luggage had been collected, people were departing, and it was then that Judy became aware of the man who stood watching them. Judging him to be about thirty, and over six feet in height, he stood with his arms folded across a broad chest. Their eyes met and their locked gazes held for several long moments while instinct told her that this was Ryan Ellison.

'A man who stands out in a crowd', Hilda Simmons had said, and Judy could only agree that he would make any girl look twice. But she hadn't expected him to be *quite* so handsome, and as he came towards them her legs suddenly felt weak and shaky. Olive-green eyes swept over her, and when he spoke it was with a deep, vibrant voice that fitted in with the rest of him.

'Is it possible you're Mrs Fulton and that this lad is Robin Bryant?' he queried.

It took her a moment to gather her wits. 'Mrs Fulton? No—I'm Judith Arledge. But this is Robin... I presume you're Mr Ellison?' As he nodded she went on to explain, 'Mrs Fulton was unable to make her visit to Napier, so Mrs Simmons arranged with me to bring Robin to you. Didn't she tell you about this change of plan?'

His tone became crisp. 'Indeed she did not.'

Observing his sudden scowl, she said, 'Is there a problem with that?'

'It's possible—unless you have friends in Napier with whom you can stay. However, we'll discuss it later. I presume you have suitcases?' He lifted Judy's cabin bag, then led the way to where the main luggage was to be collected.

Holding Robin's hand, she followed meekly, the problem being easy to guess. Mrs Fulton, she realised, would have left the boy with this man and then gone on her way, whereas she herself expected to stay with the lad at least for one night. But this, from the sound of his tone, did not suit Ryan Ellison, and suddenly Judy felt very forlorn and unwanted. Depression settled upon her as she identified their two suitcases, but she tried to shake it off by telling herself she was overreacting.

A short time later they were seated in a dark green Range Rover, little being said as Ryan drove them round the harbour, where yachts rested in the calm waters of the Napier Sailing Club's marina. Beyond the masts several fishing boats lay at anchor, and after passing a small shopping area they were rewarded by the sight of Hawke Bay, its wide, circular wave-crested expanse rimmed by distant coastal hills. On the seafront ahead of them lofty Norfolk pines rose from a long grassy verge bordering the road. And across the road from the trees stretched a row of houses, their windows glistening from the rays of the late westering sun.

Ryan stopped the vehicle in front of a wide, white two-storey house that faced the bay. A garage formed part of its base, and instead of a garden the frontage had been paved, to form a parking area between the house and the road. It was large enough to accommodate several cars, its austerity softened and made colourful by tubs filled with winter-flowering pansies, anemonies in bud and shrubs of red japonica that stood in brilliant contrast against the wall.

He switched off the ignition, but instead of getting out of the Range Rover he turned to stare at Judy. 'Miss Arledge—you've not yet explained your situation,' he reminded her smoothly. 'Do you or do you not have plans for your accommodation in Napier?'

She almost quailed beneath the hardness of his tone. 'No—I'm afraid I haven't—'

His lips tightened. 'You mean you're expecting to stay with me? Is that what you're trying to say?' The question was rasped.

'If—if you'll have me,' she returned in a small voice.

'Well—I must say this is an unexpected turn of events,' he admitted bluntly.

Her delicate brows rose as she met his gaze with frankness. 'I'm well aware that something about me niggles at you, Mr Ellison, but I'm darned if I can work out what it can be—or what I've done to merit your antagonism?'

His dark brows drew together. 'Please understand that it's nothing personal. It's just that I didn't think I'd be expected to offer hospitality to a girl such as yourself.'

'There's something *wrong* with me?' Her eyes flashed at him indignantly, widening until the reflection from her deep blue padded rain-jacket made them glitter like sapphires.

'Yes—plenty,' he snapped. 'You're too damned attractive to be staying in a house alone with a man and a small boy. I don't have young women living with me—and I intend to keep it that way.'

She spoke softly as light dawned. 'I see. You have a girlfriend who would object?'

'Not exactly.' His tone had become terse. 'However—I do happen to have a reason.'

'But we wouldn't be alone,' she reasoned. 'You have a housekeeper. Mrs Simmons said so.'

He spoke harshly. 'Hilda Simmons—or the *dragon* as I prefer to think of her—was mistaken. Kate Coster, who attends to my washing and housework, has her own cottage next door. She does not live with me.'

Judy's jaw sagged slightly. 'Oh, I see…'

Robin's voice piped up from the seat behind them. It sounded tearful. 'Don't you want us to stay with you, Uncle Ryan?'

The man sent a startled glance over his shoulder, and it

seemed as if he'd momentarily forgotten the little boy's presence. 'Yes, of course I do,' he said hastily. 'It's just that there are times when things can be inconvenient.'

Robin's voice became even more plaintive as he asked another question. 'Uncle Ryan, have you got a toilet in your house?'

'Of course, old chap. We'll go inside right away.' Turning to Judy, he said, 'We'll continue this discussion later...before you leave. Perhaps you can also throw light on one or two points that have been puzzling me.'

Before you leave, she noticed, but made no comment.

As they left the Range Rover and went towards the front door she also noticed that Ryan carried Robin's suitcase but had left her own in the vehicle. It made her realise he was adamant in not wishing to have her stay in his house, and that he fully intended to find other accommodation for her. The knowledge gripped her with a surge of disappointment, but she kept it well hidden by remaining silent as she followed him upstairs to the main living quarters.

Robin's most urgent need was attended to, and then he was shown into the smallest of four bedrooms opening off a passageway. It held a single bed with bedside table, a dressing table and a built-in wardrobe. He opened the door of the latter, and, having surveyed its emptiness, turned to the tall man with a wistful query. 'Uncle Ryan—have you got any toys?'

Ryan looked vaguely amused. 'Did you expect to find some in there?'

Robin nodded. 'Gran makes me put them away in the wardrobe. I don't want *dolls* and things for *girls*...'

Ryan flicked a glance towards Judy, then spoke in a serious tone. 'I dare say we can both do without *dolls*. I've been avoiding them for years. As for toys, tomorrow you and I shall visit the shops to see what we can find for boys.'

'And Judy—she'll come with us?' Robin asked anxiously.

'We'll see about that,' Ryan said in a noncommittal tone. 'Miss Arledge will probably be busy doing other things.'

Judy turned away to stare unseeingly through the window. It was easy to guess at what this autocratic man considered she'd be doing. No doubt winging her way back to Christchurch on tomorrow's first flight. She bit her lip as she again became gripped by a sense of having been rejected. Then came frustration, because she was unable to see what to do about it.

Of course, if she returned to Christchurch so rapidly she'd be doing exactly as the dictatorial Hilda Simmons had decreed. But she hadn't visited the coastal city of Napier before, and now that she was here the desire to have a look at the place was strong. It had nothing to do with Ryan Ellison, she assured herself firmly. Her recent experience with Alan Draper had turned her off men. Although she had to admit that there was something about this particular man that interested her—something that made her feel it would be nice to get to know him a little better, if only she could find a way past his initial hostility.

Ryan cut into her thoughts. 'I can hear Miss Coster in the kitchen. She's probably making a cup of tea.' He guided Judy towards the living room, which had a dining alcove adjoining it, the latter being attached to the kitchen by an archway instead of a door.

Kate Coster came forward to meet Judy. She was a tall, gaunt woman, with straight grey hair and a small tight mouth. Her pale grey eyes blinked in surprise as they took in Judy's youthful appearance, missing nothing—not the depth of blue in her large eyes, the slight wave in her blonde hair, nor the golden lights that made it shine.

Ryan said, 'This is not Mrs Fulton, as we expected, Kate. This is Miss Judith Arledge.'

Judy smiled and held out her hand. Determined to be pleasant, she said, 'Most people call me Judy.'

Kate Coster ignored her outstretched hand and spoke bluntly. 'Well, I must say you're not what I expected. You look as though you're still in the sixth form, or maybe just out of it.'

A cool smile touching his lips, Ryan explained, 'Kate was a school teacher before she reached the retiring age.'

Kate nodded. 'Yes, indeed. I know exactly how to handle children, especially the naughty ones.' She bent a cool gaze upon Robin, who had been staring at her with apprehension written all over his face. 'So he's to be here for the remainder of the school holidays. I hope he's a good boy.'

'Yes, of course he is,' Judy said faintly, while becoming conscious of Robin's tenseness as he gripped her hand.

'Come and talk to me, Robin,' Kate commanded, in the tone of one who would stand no nonsense.

'No—I don't want to,' Robin gasped, then slipped behind Judy and flung his arms around her while burying his face against her skirt.

Ryan became impatient. 'Just ignore him until he knows you better,' he advised Kate. 'The point is that I have a problem. I didn't think before, but it's obvious I need a woman to care for Robin while he's here. Someone with more maturity than Miss Arledge—who, as you've noticed, appears to be just out of the schoolroom.'

His words had an effect upon Judy. Her chin rose, her cheeks became flushed and her eyes flashed blue sparks as she faced him furiously. 'Mr Ellison—I'll have you know I'm more than capable of caring for Robin,' she flung at him.

'I didn't say you weren't,' he snapped.

'Then what are you saying?' Her breathing had become agitated as all her recent frustrations began to spill over. 'Please be frank so that I can understand the situation.'

'I've already told you,' he snarled. 'However, I'll spell it out again. The situation is this—I have no wish for a girl such as yourself to be living in my house. Is that clear enough?'

'Perfectly clear...although it's beyond me to know exactly what it is about me you're so afraid of,' she said with cold dignity. She took a long, deep breath. 'So, what will you do about Robin?'

'I'll appeal to Miss Coster for help,' Ryan informed her smoothly. 'I shall make it worth her while to take care of the boy.' He turned to the older woman. 'Will you agree to do so, Kate? You can either stay here or take him to your cottage.'

Kate Coster looked so startled by the suggestion she could only gape at him. Nor did she appear to be particularly pleased by it. She frowned, and although her thin lips opened, no sound came from them.

'It'll be worth your while, Kate,' Ryan pursued softly. 'You know I can be generous when the mood takes me.'

'Oh, yes, I do indeed,' Kate admitted. 'Oh...well...I...I suppose I'll do it,' she said with reluctance. 'But he'll have to be a *very good boy* and do everything I say *at once*. I shall not tolerate the *slightest* disobedience. Do you understand, Robin?' She glared at the boy menacingly.

Judy was appalled by Kate's manner and attitude. The woman's a fool, she thought. She might have been a school teacher, but this was not the way to deal with children—especially Robin—and not for one moment would she consider leaving him in Kate's care. But the boy *had* been sent to Ryan. She herself had delivered him. And because Ryan had no wish for her to be in his home the situation had become problematic.

Robin's voice rose on the air. 'I don't want to be left with *her*,' he wailed tearfully.

The boy's loud protests were ignored by Ryan. 'Well, that's settled, then,' he said with easy satisfaction. 'Kate will take over. I'm sure everything will work out well. OK, Kate—he's all yours.'

'No...no...no...' Robin shouted, while clinging even more tightly to Judy, at the same time beginning to stamp his feet.

'Stop this nonsense at once,' Kate snapped at him.

'Don't leave me, Judy,' he pleaded between gasps of weeping. 'Please, Judy…don't leave me with *her*—'

Judy began to feel desperate, her frustrations almost bursting within her as she put her arms about Robin in an effort to comfort him. She was assailed by a feeling of helplessness, and then Robin's pleadings gave rise to another question, which she flung at Ryan above the noise of the boy's weeping. Glaring at him above Robin's head, she demanded wrathfully, 'Mr Ellison—would it be too much to ask what plans you have in mind for me? As you intend throwing me out of your house, shall I be left on the road or tossed into the sea?' Agitation caused her voice to shake.

'Nothing so drastic, Miss Arledge,' he retorted coldly. 'If you'll come over to the window I'll show you where you'll be sleeping this evening. It's not far away.' He strode across the room and stood waiting for her to join him.

Judy had already noticed that most of the windows faced the ocean, and now curiosity caused her to comply with his request. Keeping her arm about Robin, she drew him with her as she went to stand beside Ryan.

He pointed towards the left, where two wide buildings were situated near the waterfront. They were surrounded by lawns and gardens. 'The first building is a motel,' he explained. 'The second is its restaurant. If the motel hasn't a vacancy I'll find you one elsewhere, and tomorrow I'll arrange for your return flight to Christchurch. There's no need for you to worry about anything. Robin will be quite all right with Kate. He'll get over his upset.'

But Ryan's words set Robin off again. Sobs shook his body as he said between gasps, 'I want to be with Judy. I don't want to be with…with that *other* one. I don't like her. She's crabby and cross.' The wails grew louder.

Kate's stern tones rose above the din Robin was creating. 'Didn't I tell you to stop this nonsense *at once*?' she scolded. 'You will come with me and have your face and hands washed.' She crossed the room and grabbed his arm, making an effort to drag him away from Judy.

But the action had dire results. Robin threw himself into one of his famous tantrums, which was something Judy had been secretly fearing. His sobs switched to loud yells as he wrenched his arm from Kate's grasp. His small fists flayed at her, then his leg swung as he kicked her on the shin with his heavy winter shoe.

Kate sprang back with a horrified shriek. *'You little brat—'* she ranted furiously. 'This is a tantrum if ever I've seen one.'

'That's right,' Judy informed her calmly. 'Robin's very good at tantrums. I've seen quite a few of them.'

'Hell's teeth—can't you shut him up?' Ryan barked at her.

His tone brought Judy's own temper seething to the top. 'Now you listen to me, Ryan Ellison,' she raged at him above the noise of the boy's gasping sobs. 'Robin is my responsibility and I won't desert him if he's not happy. If I go to that motel he comes with me. Is that understood? And you can explain the reason for it to his grandmother.' Her face flushed as she held Robin in her protective embrace.

As if by magic her words silenced the boy, who had grasped their meaning without any trouble. His tear-filled eyes gazed up at Judy imploringly as he pleaded, 'Promise, Judy... Promise you won't leave me? Promise... promise...promise...'

'Yes, darling, I promise.' She opened her shoulder bag and drew out a bundle of tissues. 'Wipe your eyes and blow your nose...there's a good boy. And don't let's have any more fuss.'

Ryan made no secret of his relief. 'At least you seem to be able to control him.'

Kate examined her shin, then demanded aggressively, 'How often do these tantrums occur?'

'Only when he feels very deeply about something,' Judy informed her. Then she sighed and went on in a resigned tone, 'If you'll pardon my frankness, I can only point out that your manner towards Robin was stern and bossy for no reason at all. It made him feel frightened and insecure. Anyone who is accustomed to dealing with young children would have realised that he's had a long and tiring day. He was up early, leaving all that's familiar, to catch a plane from Christchurch to Wellington, and then there was a wait before boarding a different plane to Napier. After all, he's only six.'

'The little man *has* had a busy day,' Ryan drawled in what sounded like a more kindly tone.

Judy pursued her efforts to make excuses for Robin. 'And that is not all. You—Mr Ellison—have made no secret of the fact that you don't want me here. That's upset him badly because I'm his link with security and all that's familiar.' She paused to take a deep breath, then went on warningly, 'If I agree to your plan and leave him here, he's likely to sob his heart out for most of the night. And when he becomes upset to that extent he's liable to wet the bed— and I'm not just talking about tears on the pillow!'

'*Bedwetting!*' The word was jerked out of Kate with a gasp of horror. 'Oh, dear...oh, dear...we can't have *that*.' She turned a pathetic face towards Ryan. 'I'm sorry...I don't think I can cope with the boy. I'm too old. I'm beyond handling children who can be as difficult as this one. I'm afraid you'll have to make other arrangements—'

'It's all right, Kate,' Ryan said irritably. 'I suppose Miss Arledge will have to stay here after all.' He sighed, as though the thought exasperated him.

Judy looked at him with disdain while wondering what on earth had made her imagine she'd like to get to know this man better. Then her tone became scathing as she said, 'Thanks a million for the charm and warmth of your invitation, Mr Ellison. However, I can assure you that staying here is the *last* thing I wish to do.'

His mouth twisted slightly as he frowned at her. 'So— what action do you intend to take?'

Feeling suddenly exhausted, Judy spoke wearily, 'If

you'll be good enough to take me to the motel, I'll stay there as you suggested—providing they have a vacancy, of course. Robin will come with me and tomorrow we'll go back to Christchurch. It's as simple as that.'

'I'm afraid it's not as simple as that,' he retorted, in a voice as hard as granite. 'The boy stays here with me. He's been sent to me and there must be a reason for it. The dragon does nothing without a reason. Perhaps you can help me fathom it out—unless you've been sworn to secrecy?'

'*Secrecy?* What utter rubbish!' Judy exclaimed, while gaping at him incredulously. 'I must say you're a strange man with some very odd ideas, Mr Ellison.'

'Am I indeed? Well, perhaps I'm approaching this from the wrong angle. Perhaps I'm being over-protective of my hermit's cave—as Kate likes to refer to this place.' He sent a mocking glance towards his housekeeper, then his manner changed as he took several steps closer to Judy and stood staring down into her face.

Speaking softly, and keeping his deep voice low, he said, 'Judy—will you try to overlook these eccentricities you see in me? I'd be grateful if you'd stay so that we can talk this over.'

So, she had suddenly become Judy, she noticed. And why was her previous attraction towards this man rearing its head again? It was something she'd have to control, and to prevent him from seeing any hint of eagerness in her eyes she turned to stare through the window as she said, 'Very well, I'll stay—but we'll talk only after Robin has been fed and put to bed.' Despite her calm assertion, the thought of spending the evening with this man made her pulses quicken.

CHAPTER TWO

RYAN turned to Kate with a request. 'Perhaps you could show Judy the food we have in the fridge? I'm sure she'll find something suitable for Robin. While you're doing that I'll bring her suitcase up from the Range Rover.'

Kate sniffed and led the way to the kitchen. 'Rather you than me with that boy,' she muttered, with a hint of sympathy.

Judy rose to the child's defence. 'He's a dear little boy and I'm very fond of him.' Then she smiled disarmingly. 'After all, most children become cross when they're tired and hungry.'

Kate sniffed again as she opened the large fridge. 'Then you'd better let him have some of this meat and vegetable casserole. You can heat it up in the microwave. Or perhaps you'd prefer to give him a plain boiled egg with fingers of toast. I'll leave you to make up your own mind about it. Goodnight.'

Judy watched her open a door in the kitchen, then make her way down a back stairway. Miss Coster, she realised, was feeling disgruntled with the world in general, but there was little that she herself could do about it. A sigh escaped her as she searched for a small saucepan in which to boil an egg. Robin, she knew, was in no state to be confronted by *vegetables*, whereas he enjoyed poking toast soldiers into a softly boiled egg.

An hour later, with a very drowsy small boy fed and put to bed, Judy was feeling more relaxed. She had renewed her make-up, and had changed into a damson-coloured dress which made her eyes seem a shade purple. She was also feeling more confident, and as she sat opposite Ryan in the living room, while sipping a delicious Spanish sherry, it was hard to believe that this was the same man who'd been so annoyed when he'd learnt she was not Mrs Fulton.

To her relief, he now appeared to be resigned to her presence, and was treating her as a normal guest instead of something untouchable that had found its way into his hermit's cave. The fact that he had no wish to entertain a young woman such as herself appeared to have been forgotten. Or had it been temporarily put on hold until he'd learnt all she could tell him?

However, he didn't rush matters, and her crystal glass had been refilled before the questions began. It was enough to make her realise that the sherry was intended to loosen her tongue, although she knew there was little she could tell him.

Ryan leaned back in his chair, his long legs stretched before him, his olive-green eyes hooded as they examined the liquid in his glass. 'OK...so tell me about the workings of the dragon's mind,' he requested lazily.

Judy laughed. 'I'm afraid it's beyond my powers to do that.'

Frowning, he said, 'As I remarked earlier, she does nothing without a reason—and as she's never gone to this extent before, I can't help wondering what it is.'

Judy shook her head vaguely. 'Apart from bronchial trouble, I can't imagine what it can be—although I can hardly believe she'd send Robin to Napier without giving *you* a reason.'

He shrugged. 'Only the one about his need for a warmer climate. Is he really bronchial?'

'To be honest, I've never noticed it,' she admitted.

Ryan continued to frown as he said, 'If it was so imperative for him to come to Napier, why didn't Verna bring him? After all, she's his mother. Or Mrs Simmons herself?'

Judy had no wish to discuss Hilda Simmons or Verna. She wanted to learn a little more about this man, whose masculinity stirred something deep within her. But she knew he expected an answer, therefore she said, 'It seems that Verna had already left for a skiing holiday a few days before Mrs Simmons decided upon this move. The snow is supposed to be really good further south, near Queenstown.'

His mouth tightened. 'I'll bet it is. It's also mighty thick on Mount Ruapehu, where I'm supposed to be skiing at present. However, this business of young Robin was thrust upon me.'

She felt perturbed. 'Are you saying you've had to forgo your own holiday?'

'That's it exactly.'

'Why didn't you refuse by explaining it was inconvenient?'

'Because I was reminded that I *owed* her, and that I *owed* Verna. It had a strong smell of blackmail about it, but I decided that if the dragon imagined I was in their debt I would prefer to be free of it.' He sipped his sherry, his eyes slightly narrowed as he went on, 'Do you ever get the feeling there's more to a situation than meets the eye? That's how I feel about this. There's something I just can't put my finger on. Are you sure she didn't say anything else?'

His last words jerked Judy's memory. 'Well…she did say she thought Robin would be safe with you.'

'*Safe?*' He sat up straight and stared at her. 'What did she mean by that? Safe from what, may I ask?'

Judy shook her head. 'I haven't a clue. I asked, but she brushed the question aside.'

'Well, that settles it,' he rasped irritably. 'The dragon has definitely got some plot simmering.'

The statement confirmed Judy's own thoughts, but all she said was, 'Verna will probably be able to explain…when she arrives.'

His face became a mask. 'Verna is coming here?'

'Of course. Didn't her mother tell you? She'll come to fetch Robin at the end of the school holidays. It'll probably please you to learn that I was ordered to return to Christchurch almost at once.'

'So I'm likely to have Verna here instead of yourself?'

She nodded. 'Perhaps sooner than you expect.' How did he feel about that? she wondered, covertly watching his face and hoping for a reaction to the thought of Verna's arrival. But his expression remained unfathomable, and she then tried to tell herself that the question had no real interest for her. Or did it?

After that a silence hung between them, until she glanced at her watch and was amazed to see how the minutes had slipped by. A hunger pang told her it was time she ate, and hesitantly she said, 'I've no wish to appear to be taking over your kitchen, but—would you like me to do something about the food Miss Coster has left in the fridge?'

Ryan took a hasty glance at his own watch. 'Yes, it's time we had supper. Let's do things together. I'll find cutlery and tablemats while you put whatever you wish into the microwave.'

She stood up and moved towards the kitchen. 'Let's do things together', he'd said. It sounded pleasant, but of course she knew that he meant nothing of a familiar nature, and the sooner she controlled her wayward thoughts the better. Remember Alan Draper, she reminded herself. All men are the same.

As he took plates from kitchen cupboards he said, 'While you're here you'll be attending to meals, so as far as the kitchen is concerned—it's all yours.'

'Thank you—I'll take care of it.' She smiled while studying which elements to switch on beneath the previously prepared carrots, Brussels sprouts and potatoes—the latter to be mashed.

He came to her aid, standing close enough for his arm to brush her own as he pointed out the various heating areas on the shiny black ceramic stove-top. It caused her to catch her breath, but she gave no sign of her racing pulses as she murmured a faint, 'Thank you.'

If he noticed that her colour had risen slightly he ignored it by saying casually, 'I must say you're very good with Robin. A real little mother, in fact.'

Praise from Ryan was unexpected. It caused her colour to deepen.

He went on, 'I was impressed by your care in making sure his teeth were cleaned before bedtime.'

A shaky laugh escaped her. 'That's because I was a dental nurse. You could say I'm very tooth-conscious.' She paused, then went on ruefully, 'You'll notice I said *was* a dental nurse.'

'You were made redundant?' he asked, while eyeing her sharply.

'Not exactly.' She spoke with quiet dignity. 'Until recently I worked for a dentist who had a one-man practice. The poor man died from a brain haemorrhage. His death put me out of a job, and so far I haven't found another.'

Judy sighed while recalling the morning she'd been phoned by a tearful newly widowed woman and given the sad news. She'd been told to cancel all appointments, then shut the door and go home. Later she'd assisted by settling accounts and making an inventory of all surgery equipment.

'I don't suppose dental nurse jobs are very thick on the ground,' Ryan said, while watching the shadows of sadness linger on her face.

'They're not...that's why I was free to bring Robin to you. But that's enough about me. You can't possibly be interested.' Then, feeling a change of subject was indicated, she said with sincerity, 'I'm sorry your holiday has been disrupted—although there's nothing to stop you from keeping to your plans. Robin and I would be all right staying here, so long as you don't object to us occupying your house while you're away.'

He said nothing while opening red wine and placing it in a bottle-holder. Then his mouth tightened as he remarked in a mocking tone, 'You sound as if my absence would be preferable to my presence.'

'It wouldn't matter to me one way or the other,' she responded coolly, while knowing this to be a lie.

He met her blue-eyed gaze steadily. 'Aren't you forgetting the small matter of the boy being *safe* with me? While you're both in Napier I intend to remain close.'

Judy's smooth brow wrinkled as she put portions of the casserole into the microwave. 'I'm still unable to understand what Mrs Simmons meant by that,' she admitted.

'Me too—but you can bet that the dragon had something in mind. She's very astute.'

Judy did not pursue the subject. She knew Hilda Simmons well enough to realise that her neighbour was inclined to dramatise and exaggerate most situations. Nor did she wish to mentally dwell upon the older woman, and in an effort to clear her thoughts she found herself wishing that the present amicability between herself and this man could be a little deeper than the mere surface.

A short time later, while serving him with food at his own table, she began to enjoy herself. It was like being his hostess, and she became aware of a small, happy glow of excitement within her. Despite his initial antagonism there was something about him that appealed to her. The shaded lights gave an aura of inscrutability to his clean-cut features, and she wondered about the direction of his thoughts. Was it possible they'd ever rest upon herself with any degree of friendship? Or was he even now happily contemplating the thought of Verna's arrival?

As if to confound her, he raised his wine glass and said, 'Here's to our better acquaintance.'

Automatically she raised her own glass while repeating his words. Did he mean them? she wondered. In an effort to clear the confusion from her mind she stared through the alcove window to where the full moon hung like a silver dollar over this tranquil corner of the South Pacific Ocean. Darkness had now fallen, and the curve of the bay was brilliantly outlined by house and streetlights situated round the shore. Close at hand, and below the window, cars sped along the seafront road the muted swish of their passing making the room seem like a haven of peace.

He said, 'You've become very quiet and thoughtful. What's put you in this mood?'

She raked in her mind for a logical reply, but could only come up with, 'You spoke of our better acquaintance—but you're ahead of me. You know much more about me than I know about you. It's hardly fair.'

His dark brows rose. 'Didn't the dragon give you a running commentary on my entire life?'

'Why would she do that?' Judy said carefully, knowing it would be unthinkable to tell him what Hilda Simmons had said concerning his land activities—or that she considered he should have married Verna years ago.

He helped himself to more mashed potatoes. 'Well—if you're really interested—I grow food for export.'

'What sort of food? Unless you think I'm prying...?'

He paused, as though wondering where to begin, then, staring into his wine glass he said, 'I grow apples for export to the UK. Buttercup squash to go to Japan. There are acres of sweetcorn, where the cobs will end up frozen or in cans, also green peas that'll receive a similar fate. There's a large area of grapes, which will go to this country's wine-makers, and in a couple of months' time the asparagus cutters will arrive at dawn each morning to harvest the spears coming through the ground.'

Judy's mind boggled as Hilda's words flashed into her memory. 'You must be a...a positive land baron,' she exclaimed, the words just slipping out.

He regarded her through narrowed lids. 'Land baron? That's what Hilda Simmons always says... Are you sure she didn't discuss me?'

Judy brushed the veiled accusation aside by asking, 'How do you manage all these areas?'

'Each section has its own manager, who is an expert in that particular line. He employs whatever staff he needs. We hold manager meetings to discuss procedure, like ro-

tation of crops and the fertilisation of the soil. The ground
has to be fed, you understand.'

She watched his lips as he spoke, noticing the sensuous
lines of his mouth. He'd know how to kiss a girl, she found
herself thinking, then dragged her thoughts back to a more
even keel by saying, 'I must say you seem very young to
have become a land ba— I mean to have acquired so much
land.'

Ryan shrugged. 'I'm a mature thirty-two,' he informed
her. 'Nor does the credit for land ownership rest with me.
About a hundred years ago one of my paternal ancestors
bought arable land when it was much less costly than it is
today. It's been passed down from father to son, some of
whom added to it. After the death of my parents it came
to me. I feel it's my duty to take care of it.' A look of pain
crossed his face.

'You're an only child?' she asked gently.

'That's right.'

'What happened to your parents?' She hardly knew how
she dared ask the question, but something stronger than
herself seemed to be at work. It was like a force that made
her want to know more and more about this man.

Ryan spent several moments in silence before he said,
'They were killed in a car accident. An idiot speeding to
pass a car caused a head-on collision. It happened soon
after I'd left school, so to keep myself sane I threw myself
into farming, so that I could carry on where Dad had left
off. I felt I owed it to him.'

'I'm sorry,' she said in a hushed voice, the thought of
such an accident filling her with horror. At the same time
sympathy made her long to reach out and touch him, and
it was only with an effort that she kept her hands to herself.

Restlessly, he left the table and began to pace about the
room. 'Normally I don't talk about it...and now I'm wondering why I'm telling you,' he said, in a tone that betrayed
irritation with himself.

'Sometimes it's good to talk,' she pointed out gently.

'Please come back to the table and finish your meal.' Then, considering him thoughtfully, she went on, 'You must have spent time in Christchurch to be so well acquainted with Mrs Simmons—and Verna.'

Her reference to Verna was ignored as he returned to the table, where he said, 'My mother and Hilda Simmons were schoolfriends who always kept in touch with each other. In fact Mother was Hilda's bridesmaid when she married Hugh Simmons. He died a few years ago. During my own schooldays Mother used to take me to stay with the Simmonses. Then Hilda rang me recently and demanded that I return the compliment by giving young Robin a period beside the sea in a warmer climate. I thought I could manage, with Kate Coster's help, but you saw what happened with the boy.'

'You agreed to do it for Verna's sake?' Judy asked with insight.

'Yes—I suppose you could put it that way,' he admitted gruffly, then his lip twisted as he added almost accusingly, 'I can't believe the dragon omitted to tell you there was a time when Verna and I were fairly close.'

'But obviously it ended,' Judy observed, while avoiding a direct answer.

'By mutual consent,' he muttered in a low growl.

She looked at him reflectively. 'I think it's possible you still have feelings for Verna...otherwise Robin wouldn't be here.'

'One doesn't forget old friends,' he retorted tersely. 'Now then—do you mind if we get off this subject?'

'Gladly,' she responded with a smile, while realising that he hadn't told her what she really wanted to know. Not that his feelings for Verna were her concern, she admitted to herself. In an effort to break the awkward silence that had fallen between them, she said, 'Would you like to finish the last bit of casserole?'

'Might as well,' he said, but before she could serve it on

to his plate they were startled by cries of distress that
floated along the passage from Robin's bedroom.

'*Judy...Judy...Judy...!*'

She dropped the spoon and sprang to her feet, then raced
along the passage to find the little boy sitting up in bed
with tears streaming down his face. His body was shaking
with sobs, and as she clasped him to her she pressed his
head against her shoulder. 'It's all right, darling—I'm here,'
she assured him, with motherly love and tenderness. 'Did
you think I'd gone away? You must've been dreaming.'

'I...I thought Uncle Ryan had sent you away,' he
gasped, while clinging to her as fresh tears fell.

'In that case you were definitely dreaming,' Ryan said
from the doorway, where he stood watching Judy's efforts
to console the distressed boy.

'Have you forgotten I promised I wouldn't leave you?'
Judy asked soothingly as she reached for tissues from the
bedside table. 'Now settle down and go to sleep.' Gently
she mopped his face, then gave him an affectionate hug
before pressing him back against the pillow.

Robin turned appealing eyes to Ryan. 'Please, Uncle
Ryan...promise you won't send Judy away?'

Ryan came further into the room to stand beside Judy.
'I wouldn't even think of it, old chap,' he assured Robin,
in a voice that was slightly husky, then, unexpectedly, he
placed his arm about Judy's waist and drew her against his
side. 'Judy and I are the best of friends now. Isn't that so?'
He grinned down at her while uttering the last words.

Judy felt herself go scarlet as, for the sake of the boy,
she stammered, 'Y-yes...I...I suppose so...'

Robin sat up abruptly, his hazel eyes sparkling with interest as they stared at Ryan. 'Are you Judy's boyfriend
now...'stead of Uncle Alan?'

Judy gave a small gasp. 'I did ask you not to mention
him!'

'Sorry, Judy...' Robin looked contrite.

Ryan chuckled as he looked down into her face again.

'So he was Alan—was he?' Then he turned to the boy again and said with what sounded like sincerity, 'Don't worry, you and I both know we can't do without Judy.'

But Judy knew better than to take any notice of his words, although she was more than conscious of the disturbing influence his touch was having upon her. Apart from sending tingles through her body, it had made her blood race, and as the pressure of his arm about her waist increased she began to tremble.

Noticing it, he said, 'What's the matter? You're like a fluttering bird.'

She groped in her mind for a reason, then gave a nervous laugh. 'You can put it down to not being accustomed to having the responsibility of a small child put upon me.'

He spoke casually. 'I can help. We'll take care of him together.'

'Thank you.' There was that word again. Together.

Staring at them wide-eyed, Robin appeared to be satisfied by the sight of them standing so close to each other. He blew his nose on more tissues, then settled down beneath the bedclothes. Judy moved from Ryan to tuck him in. Robin's lids fluttered and he appeared to be asleep before they had left the room.

When they returned to the dining alcove Ryan said, 'I'll make coffee.'

Judy watched through the archway as he became busy in the kitchen, then was unable to resist a reprimand. 'You shouldn't have lied to Robin,' she said in a serious tone. 'You know perfectly well that I'm not your girlfriend.'

He carried the steaming mugs to the table. 'I didn't lie to the boy,' he said, while placing one before her. 'At the moment you're the best girl I know. I couldn't have handled him without you. I'm now well aware of that fact.'

His words sent a warm glow through her, although she felt the need to repeat her words. 'But I'm *not* your *girlfriend*.'

'Perhaps not in the sense you mean, but I'm hoping we

can start again and at least be friends. That's if you're will-ing to make the effort, of course.'

She stared into her coffee cup, well aware that she was more than willing to meet him halfway, yet she felt reluc-tant to reveal the fact. This intriguing man—this land baron whose appearance and apparent wealth probably drew women from all sides—needn't know she was ready to join the queue of ardent admirers who were willing to swoon at his feet.

His voice came reflectively. 'In any case, I dare say Robin is too young to know anything about girlfriends.'

Judy laughed. 'Don't you believe it. At the ripe old age of six Robin has his own special girlfriend. Her name is Sally and she lives nearby. She's in his class at school, and on most days she feeds him cookies at playtime, having taken one for Robin as well as for herself. It proves that the way to a man's heart is through his stomach.'

Her words lightened the atmosphere between them, but did not remove the thoughtful expression from Ryan's face. Regarding her intently, he said, 'Tell me about Uncle Alan—whoever he is. I take it he no longer exists in your world?'

'Correct.' The word was snapped out.

He lifted her left hand, then held it nearer for clearer scrutiny. 'Do I detect a pale mark on your third finger—as though a ring has been removed?'

She snatched her hand away. 'Yes. It's been returned to Alan—' She broke off, biting back further words and feel-ing infuriated with herself. Why couldn't she keep her stu-pid mouth shut?

His eyes held a spark of interest. 'Does this mean you're footloose and fancy-free?'

'Yes, it does—and I intend to stay that way,' she de-clared firmly. 'As for Alan Draper, I'm trying to forget him—therefore I have no intention of discussing what proved to be a most painful experience.'

He grinned. 'Excuse me—are you the same person who recently said that sometimes it's good to talk?'

'It depends upon the subject,' she reasoned, and at the same time she warned herself against revealing any more— because to speak of finding her fiancé locked in the arms of another woman would be too embarrassing for words.

Thinking of it now, she wondered if she'd ever get the memory of that night out of her mind. They had been at a birthday party, but had been there for only an hour when Alan had appeared to be missing from the crowded room. Judy had felt concerned for him, because she'd known he'd been drinking. However, she had not made a fuss. Instead, she'd checked through the house, and had just completed the task when the host had handed her a torch and told her to look in the cars parked along the drive.

In the back seat of one of them she'd found Alan with a redhead named Carol Reed. Judy had shone the torch in their startled faces. She had taken one glance at the di-shevelled state of their clothes, then, snatching the car door open, she'd slipped the engagement ring from her finger and had thrown it at Alan. After that she'd run home, gasping and sobbing through the dimly lit streets.

Within a short time everyone who had been at the party knew what had happened, and soon the news of it had filtered through to the rest of her friends. But when these people had rung to offer sympathy they'd merely filled her with a desire to get away and hide. And then, out of the blue, had come the request to take Robin to Napier.

Judy had discussed the matter with her parents, who considered it had come as a godsend. It would give her something else to think about, and if she decided to find herself a job in that North Island city they would quite understand. In fact, it might give her a new lease of life.

Dragging her mind back to the present, she became aware that Ryan was observing her face through narrowed lids. She feared he was reading her expression, and this became evident by his next words.

'This painful experience—I have a suspicion you're living it all over again?' he suggested, with a hint of unexpected sympathy. 'I also suspect that whatever happened still hurts.'

She nodded, finding it impossible to speak as the memories continued to jab at her.

'This man—do you think he'll follow you to Napier if he happens to learn where you are?'

'I hope not. I don't want to see him again—*ever*.' The last word was spat with vehemence.

Ryan regarded her with concern. 'In that case you'll have to take care you're not caught on the rebound,' he warned. 'If a handsome stranger comes along and is particularly nice to you—you might fall flat at his feet. Metaphorically speaking, of course,' he added with a twinkle in his eye.

'That's most unlikely,' she retorted coldly. 'Just as you appear to be allergic to women, I'm in a similar frame of mind concerning men. At the moment I look upon them as being anything but trustworthy.'

'Thank you very much,' he growled. 'Not even present company excepted, I notice.'

She decided to be frank. 'I just feared you might be referring to yourself as the handsome stranger,' she said, while giving a light laugh to soften her words. At the same time she hoped he'd feel assured she had no intention of setting her sights on himself.

His face remained inscrutable as he said, 'I can see your hurt has gone very deeply indeed. It puts you into the dangerous state of being thoroughly vulnerable—so I'm warning you again to watch your step.'

'I'll do that,' she informed him gravely. 'Thank you for your concern, even if it is only your imagination that tells you so much about me.'

'It's not imagination,' he told her quietly. 'I've watched you with the boy, not only in the airport lounge, when you were unaware of it, but also since you've been here. It's been revealing. It's easy to see you're an affectionate and caring person, but you're also one who needs to be loved in return. That's what will make you easy prey, or—as I said—*vulnerable*.'

She looked at him thoughtfully, then dared to ask, 'What about you, Ryan? Are you so emotionally under control that you prefer to live entirely without female company?'

He gave a faint snort. 'Who says I live entirely without female company?'

'It's the impression you've given me.'

'Then allow me to correct it. When I need a woman I can always call on Cynthia.' The statement came out casually.

Her eyes widened. 'Cynthia...?' Hearing him mention the name of a woman had given her a shock.

'Cynthia Birch. She's a friend who lives at Te Pohue on the road to Lake Taupo. When I go fishing at Taupo, or skiing on Mount Ruapehu, I usually call in and have coffee with her. She's inclined to rely on me for advice concerning her financial affairs.'

'She's fortunate in having someone such as yourself to guide her.'

'Well—it's only been since her divorce.'

'I see.' She stared down at her empty plate.

'Are you sure about that? Is there anything else you'd like to know?' he drawled, while watching her from behind hooded lids.

'Not particularly,' she returned in an offhand manner, at the same time knowing this to be a lie. In fact there were several points now jumping about to arouse her curiosity, but they were not questions she felt could be asked—at least not on such short acquaintance. They'd be sure to bring forth a snub strong enough to ruin the delicate amicability that had sprung up between them.

Exactly how deep was his friendship with this woman? she wondered. And then there was the question of Verna. Did he still have any depth of feeling left for her? 'One doesn't forget old friends', he'd said, and Judy wished she knew what had come between them to end their romance.

And then another question that had often simmered in Judy's mind returned to niggle at her. It concerned the identity of Robin's father. Did Ryan know of his whereabouts? She had never set eyes on the elusive Mr Bryant, nor was his name ever mentioned. Not that it was any business of hers, of course, although she had often wondered if Verna, as a single parent, was using a fictitious name for the sake of appearances. But now that Robin was going to school he'd soon be asking questions for himself, especially on sports days and at break-up time, when the other boys produced their fathers. Where was *his* father? he'd soon be wanting to know.

Even as she pondered this question Judy looked at the man sitting at the table. The rays from the nearby standard lamp fell on his thick auburn hair, highlighting the gleam of red in it, and she was reminded of similar glints of red in Robin's hair. Startled, she was forced to wonder if Ryan could be the boy's father—was this why Hilda Simmons had sent the boy to Napier? Did she hope that father and son would find a mutual bond, so that when Verna arrived matters could be brought to a successful conclusion?

The thoughts swam about in Judy's mind until suddenly she told herself she was being stupid. She was jumping to conclusions and assuming a situation which probably didn't exist. If Ryan was Robin's father she felt sure he would have acknowledged him years ago—although why she had such faith in his integrity she was unable to say. It was just that he seemed to be an honest person who meant what he said—someone who was totally different from Alan Draper.

She was so lost in her thoughts she almost jumped when Ryan raised his hand to run a long tanned forefinger down her cheek. His touch sent a tremor through her body and her face flushed.

His eyes glinted as he observed her reaction, then his

voice became a low murmur as he asked, 'Is something worrying you?'

She forced herself to meet his gaze. 'Why do you ask?'

'Because you've been silent for several long minutes and I've been watching the changing expressions on your face. They've made me wonder if you're concerned for your safety in this house.'

She caught her breath. 'You mean from you? No…it hadn't even occurred to me.'

His dark brows drew together. 'Does that mean you consider me to be a sexless wimp?'

She gave a faint smile, while allowing her eyes to rest upon his sensuous mouth and strong jaw. This man, a sexless wimp? Not in a thousand years would he qualify. Then she said, 'No…I feel quite safe because I suspect you've no wish for me to rush screaming to Miss Coster. Besides, you need me here to take care of Robin.'

He spoke gruffly, 'Well, there's a lock to your bedroom door in case you begin to feel jittery about my intentions.'

Later, when she went to bed, she didn't even bother to turn the key. There was no need, she assured herself. She held no attraction for him—nor did he hold any attraction for her. Well, maybe that wasn't quite true, but she'd fight against it because she was finished with men and had no intention of looking at another for a long, long time. As for being caught on the rebound—huh! *That* would be the day! He must think she was a complete idiot.

CHAPTER THREE

NEXT morning Judy was awakened by the sound of Robin's high-pitched voice coming from the kitchen. She sprang out of bed and shrugged herself into a wrap, made a quick visit to the *en suite* bathroom, and, having raked a comb through her blonde hair, hurried to the kitchen where she found Robin enjoying a plate of porridge.

Standing beneath the archway, and hardly able to believe her eyes, she exclaimed, '*Porridge*—my goodness, wonders will never cease.'

Ryan said, 'I didn't have any cereal that snapped, crackled or popped, which I'm told he usually demands.'

Robin licked his spoon. 'This is good. It's better than that stuff Gran makes. Uncle Ryan says if I eat porridge every morning I'll grow up to be just like him.'

Just like him. The words clicked in Judy's mind, seeming to confirm her thoughts of the previous evening.

Ryan sent her a wink while spooning marmalade on to buttered toast. 'The secret lies in raw sugar and creamy milk. Would you like to try some? It takes only three minutes in the microwave.'

'No, thank you. Tea and toast is all I ever have for breakfast.' Then, suddenly conscious of her appearance, she added hastily, 'I'd better go and get dressed.'

Ryan spoke quickly. 'No...don't go. I like you as you are. There's something homely about a girl in a wrap and slippers.' He poured a cup of tea for her, then moved to put two slices of bread in the toaster. 'We didn't wait for you,' he went on. 'We thought it possible you needed the extra sleep.'

We, she noticed. It was almost as though he was begin-

39

ning to acknowledge Robin and himself as a unit. Strangely, it gave her an intangible feeling of being left out, but she brushed it aside and spoke casually. 'To be honest I *was* glad of the extra sleep. Yesterday had its stressful moments.'

Ryan frowned as he demanded dryly, 'Are you referring to the welcome I gave you—or rather the lack of it?'

'Oh, my troubles had begun before that,' she admitted.

Robin sent her a morose look that also held apprehension and guilt. 'I suppose you're going to tell Uncle Ryan about me being naughty on the plane?' he queried sulkily.

Ryan assumed a shocked expression. 'You were *naughty*? What did you do? Or was it something you *wouldn't* do?' he asked with perception.

Robin hung his head. 'I wouldn't stay in my seat when Judy told me to. I kept running between the seats,' he admitted contritely.

'Up and down the aisle like a young fiend,' Judy put in. 'He was over-excited by being on a plane for the first time.'

Robin became defensive. 'I was trying to make the plane go faster,' he explained. 'It didn't seem to be going very fast.'

Ryan was amused. 'No doubt it got up speed with the help of your efforts?'

Robin looked at him blankly. 'I don't know. A man put his arm out and stopped me. He pulled me into an empty seat beside him and we talked until the lady in uniform told me to go back to my own seat and fasten my seat belt.'

'So what did you talk about?' Ryan asked with undisguised curiosity.

'We talked about Judy,' Robin admitted with childish candour.

'*Me…?*' Judy demanded indignantly. 'What did he want to know about me? I'd never seen the man before.'

'He wanted to know your name,' Robin informed her. 'He said he thought you were *very pretty*.'

'Nothing wrong with his eyesight,' Ryan remarked in a droll tone.

A flush crept into Judy's cheeks but she said nothing. 'Don't allow him to talk to any strange men,' Hilda Simmons had warned. Obviously she was right, but in this case there was little Judy could have done to prevent it. Then she felt herself shrink as Robin gave out more information.

'I told him you were taking me to stay with Uncle Ryan. He asked if Uncle Ryan was your boyfriend.'

Judy's cheeks became even more pink. 'He had a darned nerve,' she snapped, while avoiding Ryan's eye.

The latter chuckled as he spoke to Robin. 'So what did you say?'

'I said that Uncle Alan was her boyfriend, but that perhaps she might swap him for Uncle Ryan.'

A gasp of fury escaped Judy. 'You said *what*?' she exploded.

Ryan held up a hand to soothe her. 'Simmer down and let him go on.' Then he turned to Robin. 'So, what else did you tell this man?'

The boy thought for a few minutes then admitted, 'I told him that I had a girlfriend and that her name was Sally and where she lives—*and guess what?* He said he knew her, and that Sally's mother is his cousin.'

Ryan spoke doubtfully. 'This is beginning to sound a little too far-fetched.' He fixed Judy with a stern eye and demanded, 'Did you speak to this man who was obviously trying to pick you up?'

His last words made her feel angrier than she already felt. 'Of course I spoke to him. Before disembarking I thanked him for bringing Robin's racing along the aisle to a halt. Believe me, with the fear of a tantrum hanging in the air I was more than grateful for his help.' She paused to draw a deep breath, then went on, 'Nor do I think it's too far-fetched for Sally's mother to be his cousin. In a country where the entire population is little more than three million people, cousins are not usually difficult to find.'

Robin's shrill voice piped up, 'What are cousins? Have I got any cousins?'

Judy smiled at him. 'I'll leave Uncle Ryan to explain while I shower and dress. He's known your mother for a long time—so he should be able to tell you *all sorts of things*.' The glance she flicked at Ryan was full of significance.

Ryan turned to regard her with a penetrating stare. She knew he was about to ask what sort of things she had in mind, but before he could do so she hurried away to her room.

A few minutes later, as she stood beneath the soothing waters of the *en suite* shower, she recalled Ryan's care and attention to Robin at the breakfast table. *Fatherly* was the word that sprang into her mind, and then the boy's own words leapt to join it. *'Uncle Ryan says if I eat porridge every morning I'll grow up to be just like him.'*

'Is that a fact?' Judy murmured her thoughts aloud. 'So how does Uncle Ryan know you'll be just like him? Surely the answer is clear. It's because he's your father, m'lad. That's why your grandmother has sent you here to await your mother's arrival…and then…?'

Judy turned off the taps and began to towel herself vigorously. Again she warned herself that there was too much guesswork going on in her mind, and if she had any sense she'd just take each day as it came. She'd enjoy Ryan's company while she could, and when Verna arrived she'd leave, with the hope that Robin had found his father.

When she returned to the kitchen she discovered that Ryan had cleared the table and tidied the worktop. And, although she waited for him to pursue the subject of why she expected him to have knowledge of Robin's relatives, he failed to do so. Instead she became aware of his interest focusing upon her own appearance, his eyes resting on her blonde hair before lowering to gaze at the rounded mounds of breasts beneath her dark red jumper.

'I suppose you know you're looking most attractive,' he remarked in a low voice. 'The men will be goggle-eyed.'

'Thank you.' She savoured the compliment while hoping her inner pleasure didn't show too much. 'They'll be here for a meeting?'

'No. They're pruning apple trees at one of the orchards. It happens during winter between leaf-fall and bud-burst. I'm taking Robin with me while I check their progress. You'll come with us to keep an eye on him,' he stated firmly. 'I hope you won't be too bored.'

The request to accompany them had come as an order rather than as an invitation, and for one mad moment she thought of refusing him. However, she decided to let the niggle pass. As for *boring* her—he must be joking. And to hide her eagerness to see part of his domain she spoke with quiet dignity. 'Of course I'll come…if you want me.'

If she'd expected a response to her last words she was to be disappointed, because he merely regarded her in silence, his frown indicating that something about her disturbed his peace of mind. But before she could utter a query Robin, who was hopping impatiently from one foot to the other, tugged at his sleeve.

'When are we going, Uncle Ryan? Can we go *now*?'

Judy spoke to the boy. 'Have you cleaned your teeth? Have you been to the toilet…?'

Robin shook his head. 'Aw, Judy… Uncle Ryan and me…we gotta go out in the Range Rover *right now*.'

She spoke with gentle firmness. 'You're not going *anywhere* until you've done those things—and don't forget to wash your hands.' Then, as the little boy ran towards the bathroom, she turned to Ryan with an apologetic smile. 'I'm sorry to cause this delay, but these things are important.'

'Yes, of course they are. Don't worry, your efforts are

not wasted. I'm really *most* impressed.' His mouth twisted slightly and the words came mockingly.

Their tone jarred on her, causing her eyes to widen into a glare of sudden anger. 'Are you suggesting I'm deliberately trying to impress you?' she almost hissed. 'If so, you're very much mistaken. I'll leave that to Verna—' She stopped abruptly, appalled by what she'd said.

He eyed her narrowly. 'Verna, huh? She's coming here to impress me, rather than to just collect Robin? Well, now…that's most interesting.'

Judy shook her head in a helpless manner. 'Please forget what I said, because I really don't know—'

'You must know something to have made that remark,' he cut in, his tone like granite. 'Why do I get a strong smell of the dragon's breath? Is this some of her scheming?'

Her slim shoulders lifted slightly. 'I suppose it's to do with why she sent Robin to you. I don't think he'll be long,' she added, hoping to get off a subject that was making him scowl.

'There's no hurry; I'm not yet ready to leave. Last evening Kate was in such a tizz she forgot to take her wages. I thought I'd drop them in to her in case she needs it. I'll probably stop and chat for a few minutes.'

Watching his athletic form descend the back stairs, she decided he had an unusually kind nature, and that few men would be so thoughtful. There was also a controlled strength about him, and suddenly she began to look upon his dominance as a gift of clear thinking, which enabled him to make the right decisions. But he was not meant for her. He was meant for Verna, she felt sure, and sooner or later they'd make up their differences. And then Robin would have a father.

Sighing, she closed the back door, and at that moment the phone rang. She went into the living room, lifted the receiver and gave Ryan's number. Her answer was greeted by a momentary silence before a female voice from the other end said, 'Is Ryan there, please?'

'No—I'm afraid he's out for a short time.'

The voice said, 'Is that you, Kate? It doesn't sound like you.'

'It's not Miss Coster. It's Judy Arledge speaking.'

'*Judy Arledge?*' The caller's voice sharpened. 'May I ask who you are and what you're doing in Ryan's house while he's absent from it? I don't recall him ever mentioning a Judy Arledge.'

'I've come to stay with him for the rest of the school holidays,' Judy explained rather inadequately, while feeling there was no need to go into details for this unknown person.

'The rest of the school holidays—but there's over a week to go.' The words came faintly, yet held a hint of agitation. 'Are you a school teacher? Am I right in assuming you're *Miss* Arledge?'

'Yes, you're quite right. May I ask who's speaking so that I can tell him you rang?'

'Indeed you may.' The caller's tone sharpened again. 'It's Cynthia Birch speaking. Ryan and I are *very close* friends—and I can hardly believe he has a...a single woman staying in the house with him. He's always been adamant in his refusal to do so—so how did you manage it, Miss Arledge?'

Something in her tone jarred upon Judy. Or was it the fact that Cynthia Birch had claimed to be *very close* to Ryan? 'I'm sure Ryan will fill you in with any details you wish to know—' she began.

Cynthia's voice rang with determination. 'If you don't mind, I'd like to know a few of them *now*. Where have you come from?'

Judy answered politely, 'From Christchurch.' And before more questions could come she added quickly, 'I'll tell Ryan you rang. Goodbye.' She replaced the receiver.

She hadn't actually hung up on Cynthia, but it had been near enough to make her feel guilty. After all, why should she care if this woman and Ryan were *close*? It shouldn't concern someone like herself...someone who was *finished* with men...and in an effort to convince herself she almost muttered the last thought aloud.

The question was still niggling at her mind when Ryan returned. She was in the living room when he walked in the back door, and for several long moments they just stood and looked at each other through the archway. The expression on his face was inscrutable, and as slow strides began to take him towards her she became conscious of a strange fluttering in her breast.

To control her nerves she drew in a deep breath, then spoke calmly. 'There was a phone call while you were out.'

He stopped in his tracks to stand very still. 'Did you get a name?'

'Yes—she said to tell you that Cynthia Birch rang.' Judy swallowed, but said nothing further, while watching for a reaction of some sort. How would he cope with both Cynthia *and* Verna—when she arrived? As for herself—it seemed clear that she wouldn't stand a chance.

A short time later they were in the Range Rover, which sped along a country highway where stands of evergreen trees gave shelter from winter southerlies, and where the bare wood of golden willows made splashes of orange-yellow beside streams. Away to the west the high Kaweka Mountains were thickly coated with snow, their dazzling whiteness giving evidence of winter.

They passed numerous orchards, flanked by rich dark acres which were being ploughed for the sowing of new crops, and just as Judy was wondering when they'd reach Ryan's land he reduced speed to turn into an extensive block of leafless fruit trees. It was sheltered on all boundaries by rows of tall, closely planted Lombardy poplars, the leaf-buds on their upswept branches already beginning to thicken.

In the centre of the orchard stood a large packing shed, and as they followed a metal road towards it Judy could see men up ladders working among the bare branches. She noticed that all the inner wood was removed, to keep the tree goblet-shaped, then guessed it was to allow the sunlight to reach the centre of the tree.

When they reached the shed, a man who was working nearby descended his ladder and came towards the Range Rover. Ryan introduced him as Bill, his orchard manager. Their talk lasted little more than ten minutes, and when it was over Ryan led Judy and Robin into the shed, where the latter immediately voiced disappointment.

Gazing about the vast interior, he spoke reproachfully. 'Uncle Ryan—there are no apples in here. I thought there'd be lots of apples.'

Ryan spoke in a kindly tone. 'Son...you're too late to see the apples—and the trees are all having their winter sleep.'

Judy sent him a rapid glance. *Son?* She permitted herself an inward smile. Sooner or later he'd give his secret away completely.

Ryan went on, 'All the apples have gone to the Apple and Pear Marketing Board. They are the people who attend to the selling of New Zealand pip fruit. Right now the apples from this orchard will be on sale on the other side of the world.'

He then went on to explain how water was used to float the apples out of their bins on to the belts, and how, at the sorting tables, every apple with the slightest blemish was discarded. Guiding them to various sections of the shed, he showed them where the packers placed the apples in cartons.

'They're paid by the carton, therefore they become very fast,' he told Judy. 'After that the fruit goes to the Apple and Pear Board's cool stores, to await shipment from the Port of Napier.' Turning to Robin, he said, 'Now then, son, how much of this shall you remember when you get home? Or will it be forgotten?'

Judy failed to catch Robin's mumbled reply. Staring unseeingly through the shed's wide opening, she thought,

There it is again. *Son.* Was it merely a figure of speech? Or was it a slip of the tongue? Not that it mattered, of course. It was just that she'd like to know the truth.

Half an hour later they were almost home when Ryan made a change of direction by turning the Range Rover towards the city. A road took them on to the sea-fronted Napier Parade, with its long line of Norfolk pines, and from there a short walk took them into the shopping centre. A store specializing in toys was soon found, and there Ryan asked Robin what he'd like to have.

The boy looked up at him in awed amazement. 'Can I have *anything*?'

'Anything you like.'

Robin's eyes widened as he stood gazing about him in fascinated wonder, and Judy guessed that he'd never seen such a display— mainly because his grandmother had kept him from such places. But now he was torn between aeroplanes, trucks and trains.

Ryan made a suggestion. 'How would you like to build your own cars and planes out of little bricks? You could build lots of other things as well.'

The boy's eyes shone. 'Could I? That'd be good!'

'Right...then come over here.' Taking Robin's hand, Ryan led him to another area of the shop. It displayed a variety of toys made from small plastic bricks in different colours, suitable for various age groups. And as Robin chose first one and then another toy, the assistant collected the boxes of bricks that applied to them.

Judy studied the expression on Ryan's face as he indulged in this buying spree. She noticed the half-smile playing about his finely chiselled mouth, and the sparkle of interest in his olive-green eyes as he examined how the bricks interlocked to form each toy. He's intrigued by the prospect of building with them, she thought, then realised he was buying as if he didn't know how to stop.

She was filled with a sudden sympathy as she suspected that perhaps he felt that he should have been doing this years ago. Was he now realising he'd missed out on a father and son relationship, and did he now intend to make up for lost time?

And Robin had also missed out. The little boy had been deprived of a loving father during his earliest years, and Judy was suddenly engulfed by an overwhelming sadness. Ryan, she felt sure, would make a wonderful father. He'd be the sort of father she'd wish to have for her own children—she knew it instinctively.

The thought startled her into realising that already she liked him rather too much—and that she'd be wise to keep a strict rein on her emotions where this man was concerned. In fact the sooner Verna arrived the better, and then she'd be able to leave the danger zone, where there was a possibility of her falling in love with this devastating Ryan Ellison. 'Take care you're not caught on the rebound', he'd warned. OK—the warning had been duly noted.

The next instant she told herself she was being ridiculous. She was off *all* men—wasn't she? Then, making an effort to brush the thoughts from her mind, she looked at the pile of packages and said, 'There's a lot to carry to the car...'

Ryan said, 'We'll not be doing that. I'll fetch the Range Rover from The Parade while you take Robin into the bookshop next door. Buy all you can find in his age group. He must get into the habit of reading,' he said, opening his wallet.

'You're very generous,' she murmured, again recognising the voice of authority and the issuing of an order. But, strangely, she didn't object to it this time. Even more strangely, she rather liked the vague sense of affinity it seemed to establish between them—but this, she knew, was only because of her association with the boy.

Watching the easy grace with which his athletic figure strode along the sheltered pavement beside the shops, she realised more than ever that his thoughts were becoming wrapped up in Robin. She herself didn't really feature in them at all, although it was possible that Cynthia Birch might occupy a corner of his mind. Or were his thoughts now veering towards Verna and all they'd once shared?

She shook herself mentally. You're being an utter fool, she chided silently. Your mind is way ahead of itself. Only time will tell if your assumptions are facts or simply the workings of your own guesswork—so just forget it and live for the day. And, with that decision made, she led Robin into the bookshop.

Within a short time of reaching home the bricks were scattered about the living room floor. Ryan showed Robin how to make a blue and yellow truck with red wheels, and as the boy's excited chatter filled the air Judy doubted that she'd ever seen him so happy. It made her steadily growing feelings for Ryan take a flying leap forward, and, unexpectedly, she was filled with a rush of tenderness for him.

Inexplicably her thoughts turned to Alan Draper, and she was amazed to find she could hardly remember his face. The discovery made her feel free of him for ever. In fact she felt so uplifted she began to feel hungry, and, glancing at her watch, she realised it was lunchtime. Was there something quick to make in the freezer? she wondered, then went to the kitchen to discover a freshly made pizza resting on the table. It had been left by Kate Coster, who had also left a note to say she'd taken Ryan's shirts home to be laundered.

After lunch, when Robin had rushed back to his bricks, Ryan said, 'This afternoon we'll take a walk along the seafront.'

Judy smiled. 'That'll be nice—but first I must thank Miss Coster for the pizza. It's a good recipe. I'd like to have it.'

'She'll be pleased about that,' Ryan said. 'But don't allow her to delay you for too long. She's a real gossip, and once she gets started she doesn't stop. By now many of her cronies will know I have a most attractive single young woman living in the house with me. And you can guess the question they'll be asking each other.'

Judy looked at him blankly until his meaning dawned, and then a slow flush began at her neck and crept up to suffuse her entire face.

His eyes held amusement as he watched it spread. 'Ah— I see you've caught on. Naturally, they'll assume we're sleeping together.'

'In that case they'll be wrong,' Judy said quietly.

'Does it upset you...if people think we're sleeping together?' The question came softly.

The penetrating stare coming from the olive-green eyes disturbed her. It made her feel she was being put through a test, therefore she answered carefully. 'Yes, because it's not the truth. I don't like lies being attached to me.' She looked at him thoughtfully, until curiosity made her ask, 'What about you? How do you feel about people knowing that your...your hermit's cave has been opened to a stranger...someone you'd never met before?'

'Surely what I do with my hermit's cave is my business?'

'No doubt, but will it affect your relationship with Cynthia Birch?'

'Why should it?'

Judy hesitated, then admitted, 'Well, she wasn't very pleased to know I'm staying here.'

His dark brows drew together. 'Did she say so?'

'No—but it came through loud and clear.'

'Did it, indeed? I'll have a word with her,' he rasped.

'No...please don't. It really doesn't matter. As soon as Verna arrives I'll be leaving. After all, she can't object to Verna being here...someone you've known for so long and who has a prior claim on you...' As the last words tumbled out she turned to look at Robin, who sat on the living room floor, his small hands pressing a red and a yellow brick together.

'You've been listening to Hilda Simmons too much!' Ryan gritted coldly. 'For your information I do not consider that Verna has a *claim* on me.'

Judy looked at him wordlessly. No claim? *What about Robin?*

He went on grimly, 'As for Cynthia, she's been hinting she'd like to take up residence in this house for some time. She's become tired of living at Te Pohue. She'd like a job and a flat in Napier, and she'd like to live here while she searches for both. The question is, would she ever find them?' he finished ominously.

'You fear *you'd* be the occupation and that you'd never get her out of your house and into a place of her own?' Judy queried.

'Exactly. It's one of the reasons my home has been kept clear of young women such as yourself,' he explained. 'When Cynthia sees you she'll be quite sure I've suddenly become hungry for male comforts.'

'Male com...? Oh...I see.' She felt confused. 'But you said there was no need to lock my door, and I believe you.'

She turned away from him to stare through the alcove window. Across the bay the distant hills were shrouded in a blue haziness, while the grey-green ocean sparkled from splashes of winter sunshine. The mere thought of sleeping with Ryan had sent another flush of colour into her face. It made her quiver inside, and sent erotic sensations through her body. Instinct told her it would be an unforgettable experience. But that was all it would be—*an experience.* Because the time for her departure from this place would come with deadly certainty.

A short time later Judy knocked on the front door of Kate's small cottage. She was ushered into the tiny sitting room, where the two casement windows gave a view of the sea, and where a gas fire burned brightly to defeat the winter chill.

The tall, gaunt woman greeted her affably. 'I'm glad you decided to come instead of just phoning,' she said. 'I'll enjoy a cosy chat, and I'm sure you will too.'

The words were sufficient to put Judy on her guard, causing her to recall Ryan's remarks about Kate's gossiping tongue. She decided to make the visit short, and, having expressed gratitude for the pizza, she thought a further apology for Robin's behaviour during the previous evening might be in order. 'He's usually a good little boy,' she tried to assure Kate.

Kate's lips thinned, giving the impression she didn't believe this for one moment. Then she asked casually, 'I suppose his mother still lives with *her* mother in Christchurch?'

'Yes. Verna has a clerical job with a large firm,' Judy told her briefly, having no intention of discussing Verna in detail.

Kate went on, 'Years ago Ryan used to tell me about her, but now he never mentions her name. There was a time when I expected them to marry, but it didn't happen. Nor did he ever tell me what had happened to finish it off.' She sent a piercing glance towards Judy. 'I suppose you've heard all about that particular episode?'

Judy shook her head. 'I know they had a relationship, but that's all I do know.' She tried to make her words sound final.

Kate's sigh betrayed disappointment. 'I was hoping you could tell me what happened to break it up.'

'I'm sorry—I haven't a clue. Nor have I any wish to know, because it isn't my concern,' Judy said pointedly, while hoping the older woman would get the message to leave the subject alone.

But it soon became clear that Kate had no intention of doing so. Gazing reminiscently into the past, she said, 'I can remember when it happened. He came home from one of his trips to Christchurch in a filthy black mood—and believe me, he took a long time to shake it off. Apart from the men on his staff he refused to see or talk to anyone. He didn't even want *me* in the house.'

'*You…?* Why would that be?'

'Because I'm a *woman*…and he was right off *women*.'

Kate took a deep breath, then went on, 'Eventually I told him that if he didn't let someone in to clean the place it would become known as the hermit's cave. Believe it or not, he said he rather liked the idea and intended to keep it that way. And, although his black mood has long since gone, the name has stuck. Nor does he allow women into the place. You've seen that for yourself.'

'I know I'm here only because of Robin,' Judy said humbly.

'And that's something else I'd like to know about,' Kate pursued with determination. 'At least you must know why Mrs Simmons sent the boy to Ryan. Do you think she's using the lad to bring them together again?'

'I...I've no idea,' Judy said, in little more than a whisper. She knew she was being pumped for information, and the knowledge annoyed her. This was Ryan's business, and not something to be passed on to Kate and her cronies. 'In any case, the affair was years ago—'

'So what?' Kate cut in. 'Ryan's assets have grown since then. He's even more eligible than he was during those days. And the fact that he hasn't married could easily make Verna think there's still a chance for a reconciliation.'

The thought was more disturbing than Judy cared to admit, yet she spoke calmly as she stood up to take her leave. 'I must be going, Miss Coster. Ryan is taking us for a walk along the seafront. Thank you again for the pizza; we all enjoyed it.'

'Getting on well, are they—Ryan and the boy?'

'Wonderfully well.' Judy told her about the purchases made that morning, but even as she hoped that this would be the last of Kate's questions she was plied with another.

It came as they reached the front door, where Kate's pale grey eyes sent Judy a direct stare. 'Do you think Robin is like his father?' she demanded bluntly.

Judy was shocked by the question, but outwardly she remained calm. And, while she herself suspected this relationship, no way would she admit it to this woman, who was possibly making a last-ditch effort to satisfy her curiosity. Instead she forced herself to return the other's gaze in a steady manner as she said, 'I've no idea. Verna is a single mother...I haven't met Robin's father.' Then she made her way along the garden path, turning at the small gateway to wave a cheery farewell to Kate, who still stood in the doorway.

When she reached home she let herself in with the key she'd been given, but instead of entering the living room, where Robin's voice could be heard reading aloud to Ryan, she went along the passage to her bedroom. It had nothing to do with not wishing to see two heads—each with a tinge of red—bent over a child's storybook.

In the privacy of her room she lay on the bed and stared at the ceiling, her thoughts mulling over the conversation she'd had with Kate Coster. Did Kate actually know for certain that Ryan was Robin's father? Had he betrayed the fact in some way? Or was the older woman merely jumping to conclusions, as she herself had been doing? But, if these surmises were correct, why hadn't Ryan and Robin been brought face to face years ago? And what had gone on to make it happen now? Something had happened, of this she felt sure.

And that word Kate had used. *Reconciliation.* It was definitely the key to the entire situation. The boy was being used to bring it about, while she herself had been used to get him into Ryan's house. No wonder Hilda Simmons had demanded her return to Christchurch before Verna arrived in Napier.

But Hilda hadn't bargained on Robin taking a dislike to Ryan's housekeeper—nor had she expected Robin to put on a performance with one of his tantrums, especially one caused by the fear of being left there without herself, Judy realised. Why hadn't Robin been told he was to meet his father? she wondered. No doubt there'd be a touching scene when Verna arrived.

It was then that Judy acknowledged her own emotions

to be in a state of chaos. Despite Robin's moments of bad behaviour, she felt a genuine fondness for the little boy. She longed to see him with parents who were *together*— but the thought of Verna's arrival ruining her own brief encounter with this man of strength and virility filled her with dismay.

'You're a fool,' she muttered to herself. 'Why can't you remember you're in his house only on sufferance?'

CHAPTER FOUR

A SUDDEN burst of impatience with herself forced Judy to spring from the bed. Ryan was taking them for a walk, so she'd better do something about her face. As she renewed her make-up she told herself there was no need to look downcast even if she felt it. Her hair was given a brisk brushing, and, after shrugging herself into her deep blue padded jacket, she found Robin's coat and made her way to the living room.

Ryan stood up as she entered. 'Ah—there you are. I was beginning to wonder if you'd forgotten about our walk, or if you intended to spend the afternoon listening to Kate's gossip. Robin and I were about to set off without you.'

'I would've understood,' she said in a low voice, suspecting that he couldn't care less whether she was with them or not.

He sent her a sharp glance. 'You would've understood what, exactly?'

She hesitated, then spoke rapidly. 'That it's better to go before the afternoon becomes too chilly.'

His hands on her shoulders turned her to face him. 'Why do I get the feeling that you didn't mean that at all—that you meant something entirely different?'

'I've no idea,' she murmured, avoiding his glance by staring at the green woollen jersey covering his broad chest. Why did her heart leap whenever he touched her?

Perhaps it was her sharp intake of breath that made him release her abruptly and lead the way downstairs. But instead of going out through the front door he paused in the lower hall to say, 'I don't think you've seen my office.'

A door was unlocked, and she was shown a room furnished with a desk and office equipment, as well as several comfortable chairs and a well-stocked bar. Next to the office was a bathroom, and a small kitchenette where tea or coffee could be made. It then struck her that Ryan had actually invited her into his holy of holies, and the knowledge filled her with a warm glow.

Had Cynthia Birch been in here? she wondered. Of course she had. According to Cynthia, she and Ryan were very close. Well—just how close would be seen when Verna arrived.

Ryan went on, 'I hold staff meetings in here. That's why the front garden has been turned into a parking lot. It enables the men to get their cars off the road.'

'Yet you've managed to keep colour with that wonderful blaze of red from the japonica bushes, and the tubs of winter-flowering pansies. Anything less like a hermit's cave I've yet to see—' She broke off, feeling she shouldn't have uttered those last words.

But they did not appear to have annoyed him, and when they left the house a few minutes later he surprised her by taking not only Robin's hand to cross the road, but also her own. He's a caring man, she thought, while becoming conscious of the firm clasp of his fingers. Nor was it possible to ignore the thrill of his touch, which sent pulsating tremors up her arm and down her spine. However, on the other side of the road, her hand was hastily dropped.

The walk took them towards the Port of Napier, where a large container ship lay berthed at one of the wharves. Ryan led them to a vantage point from where they could watch much of the activity. To Robin he said, 'That's the *Barcelona*. She's being unloaded. Do you see those huge boxes being lifted on to trucks by cranes? They'll be taken to people who...'

But Robin wasn't listening. He'd darted away and was running towards the wharf.

Ryan shouted at him. 'Hey—where are you going?'

The boy paused momentarily. 'I'm going to get on that ship—'

'Like hell you are,' Ryan roared, then sped after him, his long legs enabling him to overtake Robin within moments.

Watching them from a distance, Judy waited for a tantrum to begin, but the yelling and stamping did not come. And after Ryan had spoken to the boy for a few minutes they returned to her side.

Robin looked up at her. 'We're going home now,' he announced. 'Uncle Ryan is going to show me how to build a container ship with my bricks. He says I can have a hot chocolate drink, and that you'll make him a cup of tea.'

'I'll do that gladly,' Judy said as the knowledge that she'd do anything for Ryan hit her like a bomb.

When they reached home it took only a short time to make Robin's chocolate and to watch it vanish before he was on the floor with his bricks. Ryan started him off on the ship-building process, then rose from his knees and came to the alcove table as Judy reached it with a tray bearing tea things.

Watching her pour the tea, he spoke in a voice that held a hint of command. 'Now you can tell me more about yourself. I know so little.'

It was an effort to keep her hand steady as she said dismissively, 'I'm afraid there's nothing of interest to learn about me. To you—in a few weeks—I'll be less than a fleeting memory of someone who flitted by during the July school holidays.'

'You underrate yourself,' he assured her smoothly. 'Tell me about your parents. Are they friendly with Hilda Simmons? Is your mother one of the dragon's do-gooders?'

Judy laughed. 'Definitely not. I'm afraid Mother's far too busy doing secretarial work in the company's office. She says it keeps her brain active.'

His brows shot up. 'What company is this?'

'Arledge Brothers. My father and his brothers are land developers. They buy suitable land and build on it.' Judy fell silent for several moments before she admitted, 'To be honest, my father refuses to even socialise with Hilda Simmons.'

'Wise man...but why is that?'

'Several years ago, when our house was being built, she made a special trip to his office with a demand that annoyed him. Believe it or not, she wanted the right to vet the people who'd be moving into it,' Judy said. 'Anyone whom she considered to be of ''lower class'' must be kept out—and as Dad intended moving into it himself he took umbrage. He immediately wiped her off *his* list of preferred people.'

Ryan chuckled. 'That's the dragon. She's a real snob. I can almost picture the scene. I think I might like your father. But tell me, why didn't you join the family firm?'

'Because I wanted a job away from the company,' Judy explained. 'It made me feel more independent to be away from the constant talk about land purchases, building permits and construction plans. Can you understand?' She looked at him anxiously.

'Quite easily.' Ryan's olive-green eyes had become shadowed by sympathy. 'So, the death of your employer, coupled with the difficulty of finding another dental job, plus your broken engagement, have all combined to give you a depressing time.'

'You can say *that* again,' she muttered dolefully. 'I've no wish to sound sorry for myself, but the last two months have given me my own personal winter of discontent.'

He reached across the table to hold her hand, and in a tone that offered comfort he said, 'These things pass, especially if one talks about them. It brings them out into the open and gives them the chance to be blown away. Believe me, this is something I happen to know about.' Grim lines had appeared about his mouth.

But she failed to notice them, otherwise she might have questioned him further. Instead she became fascinated by the sight of his hand holding her own for the second time. It was something she hadn't expected to see, and again she was aware of the pressure sending tingles of electricity up her arm. It caused her voice to become unsteady as she said, 'I doubt that the memory of seeing Alan with some- body else will ever be blown away by mere talking.'

'Try it and see,' he urged gently. 'No matter what has happened to one, there is always somebody else who has suffered a greater trauma. Go on...tell me.'

But she continued to stare at their clasped hands until a surge of common sense forced her to pull herself together. Don't be daft, she warned herself silently. It doesn't mean a thing. It's merely a small gesture of sympathy. Then she spoke in a low, tense voice, telling him about the party, and how Alan had been missing until she'd found him in the car with Carol Reed who, she'd been told later, had been angling to catch his attention for months.

But the memories had an effect upon her, and, as the scene in the torchlight loomed before her eyes, shock re- turned to grip her emotions. It caused a gush of uncon- trolled tears to turn her eyes into deep blue pools, but before they could overflow she snatched her hand from Ryan's grasp and fled to the kitchen. She grabbed a tissue from the box on the worktop and dried her tears.

She heard Ryan come into the kitchen and stand behind her. The feel of his hands on her shoulders sent more vi- brations through her body, and when he turned her round to face him she found herself unable to look up at him. Instead she rested her head against his shoulder, then be- came aware of contentment as she felt his arms wind them- selves about her.

There was a sudden stillness, before his embrace tight- ened to hold her closer to him, and then a finger beneath her chin tilted her face upward. His head bent, and as his mouth rested upon her own she was unable to prevent her lips from parting. Nor could she prevent her arms from creeping about his waist, and the next instant she found herself clinging to him while her breath quickened and her heart thudded against her ribs.

His action had come as a surprise, and again she warned herself it was only *sympathy*. Even so she lacked the power to disengage herself from his arms or to push him away. And as she revelled in these moments her body cried out for much closer intimacy.

His lips leaving her own to trail towards her throat made her catch her breath. His fingers in her blonde hair sent tremors quivering through her body, and as his hands descended to gently massage the muscles of her back she was sent into a blissful trance. It was only then that the alarm bells began to clang in her head. He's not for you, they seemed to say. He belongs to Verna—or at least he *should* belong to Verna, for Robin's sake.

Taking a deep, gasping breath, she tried to push against his chest. 'Ryan...please...this must stop. You probably think I'm being an idiot. I didn't want to talk about Alan, but it was you who persuaded me to do so...'

'I'm glad I did, because now I know you really have got him out of your mind...out of your heart...out of your entire system. You suffered just as I did by having your pride hurt, but believe me—it mends.'

She looked at him anxiously. 'How long did it take to know it was only your pride that was hurt?'

'As soon as I could think clearly. I knew that a person who cheats on another isn't worth grieving over.' He looked at her sternly. 'In any case, you weren't *really* in love with that fellow.'

Her eyes reflected indignation. 'What makes you so sure of that?'

His mouth twitched, betraying faint amusement. 'It was your response to my kiss. It was warm and vibrant. Your whole body sprang into life. If you'd been in deep emotional mourning it wouldn't have been like that. Shall I show you again what I mean?' His hands cupped her upturned face as he gazed into her eyes while awaiting her answer.

It came as a breathless whisper. 'Y-yes...please...'

His hands moved to sweep her against him, and as his lips brushed across Judy's mouth in a series of gentle kisses her heart began to beat faster. Her lips parted, and as the kiss deepened into one of passion she felt as though she'd melt. Trembling, and aware that her legs felt weak, her arms went about his neck, and she clung to him with even more joyous response.

At last he raised his head. 'See what I mean?' he asked in a deep, throaty voice that didn't seem to be quite his own. 'You weren't in love with Draper at all. You only thought you were.'

She bit her lip, finding speech impossible because she knew he was right. If she had truly loved Alan, how could another man sweep her towards heaven so soon? And then she was startled as the sound of Robin's voice came from the archway.

Wide-eyed and open-mouthed, he echoed disapproval. 'Uncle Ryan—*I saw you kissing Judy.* I don't kiss Sally. I don't kiss any *girls*.' He sounded thoroughly shocked.

Ryan released Judy as he spoke to the boy. 'Give yourself time, son, and you will...I'm willing to take a bet on it.'

Son. The word dragged Judy back to earth with a sickening thud. And then she became aware that Ryan was offering Robin an explanation.

'It was like this, lad,' he said. 'Judy was in need of a spot of comfort, so I was just kissing her better.'

A spot of comfort. Sympathy. His words confirmed her previous suspicion that *that* was all it had been. Nothing more—nothing less. OK—she knew where she stood, so why was she feeling so dismal?

The explanation appeared to satisfy Robin, who brushed the issue aside by voicing hopes of his own. 'Uncle Ryan, can we go out in the Range Rover again tomorrow? We haven't got a Range Rover at home,' he added plaintively.

Ryan spoke kindly. 'Yes, I'll be taking you out tomorrow.' He turned to Judy with further explanation. 'I need to check the vine fences at one of my vineyards, and then we'll go on to Te Pohue. You'll see some of the country.'

Conscious of rising spirits, Judy felt a smile light her face as she said, 'That'll be nice. Do you grow something at Te Pohue? Is it far?'

'Less than thirty miles away, but, no—I don't grow anything there. Many years ago Te Pohue was one of the staging posts for horse-drawn coaches carrying travellers over the mountain ranges between Napier and Lake Taupo. Now it's only a tiny settlement, with a pub and a small lake. Robin will be treated to a donkey ride—and we'll have lunch with Cynthia.'

'Oh.' Judy's soaring spirits crashed to earth. For some unknown reason the thought of meeting Cynthia Birch filled her with anxiety. 'Why don't you and Robin go alone…?' she began.

'Certainly not,' he cut in sharply. 'You're coming with us.' It was an order against which it would be useless to argue.

Next morning dawned with the promise of being one of the more pleasant antipodean winter days. The air was clean and fresh, the frosty chill in it being compensated for by the blueness of the sky and sea, and the dazzling whiteness of the waves breaking round the long curve of Hawke Bay.

Little was said during breakfast, and although Judy longed to know more about the relationship between Cynthia and Ryan, his expression told her nothing. Nor did he appear to be in any mad rush to reach Te Pohue. It was mid-morning before the Range Rover was making its way westward, towards the countless ridges of mountain ranges that could be seen across the bay from the house windows.

Even from the distance they had caught Judy's imagination, causing her to wonder what lay between the bluish-grey folds; however, when gazing towards them she had not realised she'd be going there to meet a woman who claimed to be Ryan's *close friend*.

Before reaching the higher hill country, the road ran through the fertile Esk Valley, where there were vineyards, citrus and other types of orchards. Ryan cruised along it, then reduced speed to turn into a large block where men could be seen working between rows of grapevines. As he left the Range Rover they came towards him, their shouted greetings and remarks indicating the good relationship he had with his staff. Then the voices faded as they moved away to examine the fences holding the vines.

A short time later they were on their way again, the road now rising to follow the contours of the pine-covered hills. In places there were steep drops, with streams far below. As the miles fell behind them the thought of meeting Cynthia Birch caused Judy to become more and more tense.

Somehow a hint of her nervousness conveyed itself to Ryan. 'You don't appear to be very relaxed,' he remarked. 'Am I going too fast for you?'

She bit her lip while raking her mind for a suitable reply. It was impossible to tell him that the thought of meeting Cynthia was making her feel uptight. He'd want to know *why*—and she'd be unable to find an answer that didn't sound as though she was looking for trouble before they'd even met.

At last, speaking in a low voice, she said, 'You're not driving too fast for me, but I wouldn't like swinging round the corners to make Robin car-sick.'

The suggestion was enough to make Ryan slow down and send an anxious glance towards the boy. 'Are you feeling OK, son?'

'*Course* I am.' Robin's reply came indignantly.

Judy said, 'I think he likes it when you call him son. I suppose it makes him feel as if…as if…' Her words dwindled away as she realised it had been an idiotic thing to say. Why had she so little control over her thoughts and her stupid tongue when she was with this man?

Ryan made no reply. He merely scowled at the road ahead.

She took a sly glance at the outline of his handsome profile, then noticed the grim expression of his mouth. Had her remark annoyed him? she wondered uneasily. Had it enabled him to guess she suspected Robin to be his son? Many times she had scanned the boy's features while searching for a likeness, but apart from the similar glint of red in their hair there was little to point to them being related. So why did this idea stick in her head?

And then curiosity forced her to ask, 'Has Verna ever met Cynthia?'

'Not that I'm aware of.' His tone was clipped.

'Then she…she doesn't know of your friendship with her?'

'No. Why the hell should she? It's not her concern…nor is it the concern of anyone else for that matter,' he rasped, while sending a sidelong glance at Judy.

She recognised the reprimand in his tone, then cursed herself for having mentioned Verna's name. After that there was silence between them until they reached the Te Pohue settlement, which nestled in a basin at the foot of high hills. There was a small lake that glistened like a gem, its shimmering reflections coming from the blue sky and the different greens of the surrounding high land and trees. A narrow gravel driveway led towards it, at the same time passing a small white timber-built cottage situated near its shore.

Ryan stopped the Range Rover beside steps leading up to a veranda. The front door opened almost immediately and a tall red-haired woman emerged. She appeared to be about Ryan's age, the slimness of her figure emphasised by a tailored sage-green trouser suit with a white blouse beneath the jacket.

The words that sprang to Judy's mind were 'elegance' and 'sophistication'. Together they gave her an inferiority complex that caused her to wonder why she'd come out in casual clothes instead of something smarter or at least more feminine. Well, it was too late to worry about it now, she

thought, while observing Ryan greet Cynthia with brief
kisses on either cheek.

Were they lovers? she wondered. If so she didn't want
to know about it. She didn't want to watch them together
or catch a glimpse of any fond glances passing between
them. At the same time she knew she couldn't remain sitting in the Range Rover, and, making an effort to pull her
thoughts together, she left the vehicle to join the group on
the veranda.

Ryan introduced them, and as Cynthia held out a limp
hand her green eyes flashed an appraising glance over Judy.
'You look very young to be in charge of a child,' she said,
in a slightly superior tone.

Judy refused to take offence as she explained, 'I'm not
in charge. I've merely brought him to Ryan—'

'Nonsense,' Ryan cut in. 'You're in charge of his needs.
You're like a mother to him—'

'While you're like a father to him?' Cynthia interrupted
sweetly. 'Really, Ryan—isn't it time you had a son of your
own?' The words came with a provoking smile.

Judy imagined she sensed Ryan stiffen, but before anything further could be said Robin piped up to voice the
priority in his mind.

'Uncle Ryan says you've got a donkey. Where is it? I
want to see it. Can I have a ride on it?' His hazel eyes
glowed with happy anticipation.

Amused glances met over his head, then Cynthia said,
'Neddy's in his paddock. Come this way and Uncle Ryan
will lift you on to his back. He's very gentle.'

They followed her along a passageway, through the
kitchen and out of the back door. From there a path led
them to where a grey donkey grazed in an enclosure. It
raised its head at their approach, then slowly walked towards them.

As they stood beside the animal Judy made an effort to
show a friendly interest. 'Do you keep a donkey for any
special reason?' she asked Cynthia.

'Only out of kindness,' Cynthia said virtuously. 'His previous owners moved away from the district but were unable to take him with them. They asked me to give him a home because nobody else would.' She paused to sigh. 'But now that I want to leave Te Pohue to live in Napier, I find I'm stuck with him. Nobody wants poor Neddy. Ryan knows exactly what I plan to do—don't you, *dear*?' She sent him a glance that was full of meaning.

Ryan made no reply as he lifted Robin on to Neddy's back. And, as he led the animal away by the halter it was wearing, it seemed as if he hadn't heard Cynthia's last words. Or had he deliberately ignored them? Judy wondered.

Watching them move towards the gravel driveway, Cynthia went on, 'How long do you intend to stay with Ryan?'

'Only until Verna arrives...'

'*Verna?* Who is she?' Cynthia demanded sharply.

'She's Robin's mother. Ryan and she are old friends,' Judy informed her. Somehow she expected Cynthia to have heard of Verna. She began to wonder just how much this woman knew about Ryan's past. Not a lot, it seemed.

Cynthia's voice held a vague tinge of agitation. 'Tell me more about this...this Verna person. Is she somebody who is *close* to Ryan?'

Judy smiled inwardly. 'I haven't a clue. Why don't you ask him?'

'That would be impossible.' The words were snapped.

'Well, they're close enough for him to have her son staying with him,' Judy pointed out casually, while turning to watch Robin's infinite joy at being given a ride on Neddy.

She noticed that Ryan also appeared to be enjoying himself. As he led the donkey along the driveway towards the highway, where they turned to come back, he was grinning broadly. And again the thought of the years he'd missed with the boy made Judy's eyelids prickle.

Cynthia broke into her thoughts by saying, 'Thank heavens for school. I mean, the boy's mother will have to get him home for the beginning of the new term—otherwise she might settle in and stay so long it would mess up my plan.'

'Your…your plan?' Judy became conscious of misgivings.

'As soon as I've found a home for Neddy I intend to rent out this cottage and move in with Ryan. I'll live with him until I've found a flat that really suits me. That's if I ever do, of course. Fortunately you've opened the door for me.'

'I have…?' Judy found difficulty in hiding her dismay.

'Of course you have.' Cynthia's satisfaction was evident. 'Until your arrival he'd been *adamant* about refusing to have a woman staying with him. But now that he's had you staying with him, he'll have no excuse to refuse me.'

'Especially as you're *so close*,' Judy was goaded to murmur.

'And especially as I intend to be even closer,' Cynthia retorted with determination.

Looking at her, Judy realised that here was a thoroughly stubborn woman who knew what she wanted and intended to get it. At the same time she had to admit that Cynthia was really rather beautiful, and that she and Ryan would make a handsome pair. So why hadn't he married her the moment her divorce had become final? Was it because of Verna?

She took a deep breath and chided herself. Stop it, you fool. You're at it again—jumping to conclusions. Still some of them could be true, she felt, while refusing to ask herself why the course of Ryan's emotions should concern her to such an extent.

Yet was there any need to ask herself this question? Didn't she know it was because the memory of those kisses in the kitchen kept raising its head to haunt her? Since those heart-stopping moments it had never been far below the surface of her mind, and even now she could almost feel his firm lips nibbling along her jawline before coming to rest on her mouth. Even now she could almost feel the pressure of his arms holding her body close to his own. Ryan, oh, Ryan, she breathed silently. Why do these memories fill me with animosity towards Cynthia—and towards Verna, despite Robin's need for a father? The last thought brought a deep sigh.

It did not escape Cynthia. The green eyes narrowed as she said, 'Are you feeling depressed? Perhaps you're missing a boyfriend and would like to go home to Christchurch?'

Judy shook her head. 'No. In any case I promised Robin I'll not leave him. I'll stay until his mother arrives.'

'When do you expect that to take place?'

'I...I'm afraid I've no idea.'

'*Really*. These arrangements sound too vague for words,' Cynthia said crossly. 'However, if you do happen to change your mind and wish to go home, I can take care of Robin. I think he'd like to be here with me—especially with Neddy to ride,' she added significantly.

Again Judy shook her head. 'I promised Robin I wouldn't leave him,' she repeated in a firm tone.

Cynthia's voice turned cool. 'Don't you mean you rather like being here—with Ryan?'

Judy's smile became full of innocence. 'Oh, yes, I'm loving it. He's already taken us to see a couple of his properties, and we've been shopping for toys and books for Robin. He's such a kind man.'

'Don't you think I know that?' Frustration caused Cynthia's lips to thin, then she went on with barely concealed impatience, 'I suppose you know your presence has completely ruined his skiing vacation?'

'Yes, I'm sorry about that.' Judy spoke regretfully. 'But he's his own boss. He can go later.'

'Can't you understand?' Cynthia demanded angrily. 'His friends are there now. *Later* won't be the same for him.'

'Oh, yes, I'm aware of that.'

'Then you should do something about it. You should follow my suggestion and allow Robin to come to me. I'll talk to Ryan about it,' Cynthia declared with unyielding determination.

The subject was brought up at lunchtime, when they sat down to a tasty fish pie served with vegetables, followed by date scones and coffee. However, as Ryan listened to Cynthia's plan, which would enable him to join his friends at the Ruapehu ski-fields, his expression became unfathomable.

'Well, what do you think?' she queried, in a voice that held a ring of confidence.

Ryan shook his head, his face becoming grave as he said, 'Thank you for the thought, Cynthia, but I'm afraid there are three reasons to prevent it.'

She was openly crestfallen, her winning smile fading as she exclaimed, 'Three reasons? What are they, for heaven's sake?'

He began to list them. 'For starters, number one is the fact that Robin has been sent to *me*, and I'll not hand him over to somebody else. Secondly, I'll not force Judy to break a promise she's made to the child. It's a bad thing to do. And, number three—my accommodation at the mountain has now been cancelled. I'm sure you'll realise the place is full.'

'I'm sure they'd find a bed for you,' Cynthia persisted, then, refusing to give up, she turned to Robin as though enlisting him as an ally. 'Did you enjoy your ride on Neddy? Would you like to come and stay with me and have lots and lots of rides?'

Robin swallowed a mouthful of scone before he said with a hint of complaint, 'Neddy wouldn't gallop for me. He would only walk.'

'But you're not ready for gallops,' Ryan explained. 'Besides, Neddy confided to me that he hadn't galloped for years, and he had no intention of doing so now.'

His words had given Cynthia an idea. 'A pony—that's

what he needs,' she exclaimed. 'I'm sure I could borrow one—so you must let him come to me, Ryan, and then Judy could go home…' Her words dwindled away as she looked at him hopefully.

Grinning at her, he reached across the table to pat her hand. 'Cynthia, old dear, you must be getting deaf. Didn't you hear my reasons for keeping Robin with me?'

Cynthia was not amused. She pouted childishly while saying, 'Please don't call me *old dear*.' Then she went on with a burst of inspiration, 'At least you could bring him out here to the pony club. There's a group of children with ponies who meet every day during the school holidays. I'll make it worthwhile for one of them to give Robin a ride,' she declared with determination. 'A few dollars and they'll all be offering their ponies.'

'I'll leave you to make arrangements,' Ryan grinned.

Later, as the Range Rover swung round corners on the way home, Judy noticed that the man sitting beside her had become very silent. She glanced at him occasionally, but he continued to frown at the road ahead, and at last she began to wonder if she herself had annoyed him in some way. Had she made a tactless remark?

Hesitantly, she said, 'You're very quiet. Is everything OK?'

There was a pause before he said, 'I was thinking of Cynthia.'

Of course—why couldn't she have guessed? And, as his admission sent her spirits plunging to zero, she managed to say in a normal tone, 'I'm not surprised. She's…rather beautiful.'

'Yes, I suppose she is.' He sent her a penetrating glance, then went on, 'When I was giving Robin a ride you appeared to be chatting quite amicably. However, as neither of you were smiling, I got the feeling that something of importance was under discussion. Am I right?'

'Yes…I suppose you are. At least, it was of importance

to Cynthia,' Judy said. It was also of importance to herself, but this was something she was unable to admit.

'Well, what was it?' he queried in a demanding tone. 'Or would that be breaking a confidence?'

'Not really, because you already know about it. You previously told me she'd like to move in with you,' Judy reminded him. 'And actually it's her plan to do so as soon as…as your house is…is free of other women.'

'Such as yourself?' he asked dryly.

'And Verna, when she comes to collect Robin.' She turned to look at him curiously. 'I was surprised to learn that Cynthia has never heard of Verna.'

'That's because I'm not in the habit of discussing her,' Ryan retorted in an abrupt tone. 'What did you tell her about Verna?' His voice hardened, as though accusing Judy of gossiping.

'Only that she's Robin's mother and that she'll be coming to fetch him,' she said defensively.

'So, when do you think she'll arrive?' he asked in a flat tone.

Judy considered the question before she said, 'At a guess, I'd say during the next few days. I'm sure she'd like to have some time with you before returning to Christchurch.' She sent an anxious glance towards him while wondering what was going on in his mind.

At last he asked in an amused tone, 'Are you suggesting there's to be a reconciliation?'

'Well, I have wondered about it,' she admitted in a small voice.

Ryan chuckled. 'In that case you'll just have to wait and see what happens.' After that the twisting road held his attention for the remainder of the drive home.

CHAPTER FIVE

THE next two days were stormy. The sky remained sombre,
the wind whipped the waves of a grey-green sea and the
rain poured as though the heavens had opened. Robin was
occupied with his books and bricks, dismantling previously
made toys in order to make fresh ones. Ryan spent hours
in his office, catching up on neglected tasks, and it was
only Judy who was at a loss to know how to fill in the
dreary days.

For a time she watched TV, then—becoming jaded with
the programmes—she switched it off and went to the window to stare at the gloomy scene. And, as boredom gripped
her, she wondered why she hadn't purchased some needlework when they'd been in town. Or, more to the point—
why hadn't she brought an unfinished piece of work with
her?

Judy was fond of needlework, and she now thought of a
tapestry picture she had begun. But the breaking of her
engagement to Alan Draper had caused her to lose interest
in it, and it had been shut away in her needlework box.
However, now that she'd got Alan out of her system, she
would have been grateful to have had that piece of work
with her.

No doubt working on it would have brought thoughts of
him to mind, but to do so without the old hurt raising its
head would have been like a healing therapy. In any case,
how could thoughts of Alan disturb her when a man like
Ryan was so near? Even as she pondered over this question
he entered the room unheard.

'Are you all right?' he asked from behind her, his eyes
taking in the lines of her smart apricot trouser suit.

74

She turned to look at him, then found herself struck by the aura of male strength that seemed to radiate from him. It was emphasised by the black jersey encasing his muscular arms and chest—and suddenly she had an overwhelming desire to be held in the comfort and warmth of those arms and against that chest. It caused her to turn away before her eyes betrayed her longing.

He came closer, then his hands on her shoulders turned her to face him. 'I asked you if you were all right. I heard you sigh. It made me wonder if you were unhappy for some reason.'

'It's just that I'm not used to being idle,' she admitted with a smile. 'Actually, I was regretting not having some needlework on hand. I should've thought of it when we were in town.'

He looked at her thoughtfully, until he said, 'Do you mean needlework as in tapestry?'

'Yes. I should've brought the half-finished work I have at home.'

His mouth twisted slightly as he queried, 'Would you be interested in a piece of half-finished work I have here? It's a tapestry cushion.'

'Somebody left it...?'

'Not exactly... Somebody threw it at me—literally.'

Curiosity forced her to ask, 'Would it hurt too much to tell me about it? Was it Verna?'

'Of course it was Verna. Who else? She was working on it when we had the colossal row which finished our relationship.' His mouth tightened as he glared at the rain-splattered window.

'What was it about?' Judy was unable to resist the question.

'The row? I've no intention of discussing it,' he snapped. 'Even the memory of it infuriated me for a long time.'

She felt contrite. 'I...I'm sorry for asking. It's not my concern.' Then she spoke with compassion. 'But...surely you've wiped it from your mind by now.'

'I've wiped the *rage* from my mind…although I can still see the scene quite vividly. I can almost hear her screeching at me to go to hell while she stuffed the tapestry and wools into a bag. Then she threw the lot at me. When it fell at my feet I remember looking at it for a few moments, then I picked it up and thanked her with exaggerated politeness. I told her I'd find somebody to finish it, then I'd use it as a reminder never to become involved with another woman. At least not seriously.'

Judy laughed. 'It's not much of a reminder when it's tucked away out of sight. Nor has it saved you from becoming close to Cynthia,' she teased.

'Who the hell says I'm close to Cynthia?' he snarled.

'Well, it's what I've been given to understand,' she said sweetly. 'May I see the tapestry?'

'I'll fetch it,' he said gruffly, then left the room, to return moments later with a yellow plastic bag. It contained a square of printed tapestry canvas and skeins of wool in various shades of sky-blue, sea-green, grey and white. There were also brown and black.

Judy spread the canvas on the table, then stared at white sails and a choppy sea. 'It's a sailing ship,' she exclaimed. 'There's not a great deal left to do.'

Ryan shrugged. 'I don't care what it is,' he said in a dismissive tone. 'It's there if you're looking for something to do in the way of needlework.'

'Thank you, I'd like to finish it. It's a pity to see so much work wasted,' she said, turning it over to examine the neatly finished off threads at the back of the canvas. Then she sat down and threaded a needle with sky-blue wool.

As she did so her mind tried to capture the scene Ryan had painted. She knew Verna had a temper, and she could imagine her throwing things. However, she found difficulty in visualising Verna walking straight back into Ryan's arms. Would they be held open to welcome her? Or would he tell Verna she was becoming more like her mother every day?

He broke into her thoughts by saying in a terse tone, 'When you leave here you may take it with you. I'd like to get it out of my house.'

When you leave here, Judy thought sadly. He'd made it clear he couldn't care less about *that*. But she was beginning to care about it, and secretly she was counting the days she thought she had left with Ryan. They were becoming precious to her.

Suppressing a sigh, she said lightly, 'When I'm home I'll look on this as a souvenir of my stay in the hermit's cave. I'll always think of this place by that name.' She looked up at him, then was annoyed to find her eyes suddenly becoming misty. Blinking rapidly, she lowered her gaze to the needle, which immediately became a blur.

Watching her, Ryan said, 'Do I detect a slight depression? You've got your needlework, yet you don't look happy.'

She ignored his remark by saying, 'To be honest, I can't understand why you haven't had it finished and made into a cushion years ago...I mean, as your protection against the female species. Isn't that what you told Verna you'd do? Kate Coster would've obliged.'

'That's easily explained,' he rasped impatiently. 'After I'd cooled down I knew I didn't need a reminder because I'd thrown myself into work. I'd become too busy to allow involvement with a woman.'

'Not even with Cynthia?' Judy dared to ask.

'Especially not with Cynthia. At that time she was still married,' he pointed out. 'I knew her husband, and that's how I met her. Their divorce is fairly recent.'

Judy spoke quietly. 'Now that she's free you'll need more than a cushion to protect you from the plan she has in mind. That's if you've any wish to be protected,' she added as an afterthought.

'Maybe I have a plan of my own.' He grinned.

'Oh...of course...you'll put it into action with Verna's

arrival,' Judy exclaimed as realisation hit her with force. 'Cynthia will see where she stands the moment she knows Verna is here to stay and that you are Robin's...' The word died on her lips.

The olive-green eyes held a glint of humour. 'Yes...? Go on—the moment she knows I'm Robin's...what?'

Somehow she couldn't bring herself to utter the word *father*. It seemed to stick in her throat, therefore she improvised by saying, 'The moment she realises you're about to take over the moulding of Robin's future.'

He looked doubtful. 'His future? Who knows what the future holds for any of us?'

Recalling Alan Draper's betrayal, she said, 'My mother says it's usually an unexpected event that alters whatever plans we have made.'

'Your mother sounds like a wise woman. I think I might like her as well as your father.'

Judy spoke impulsively. 'I know she'd like you, whereas she never liked...'

'Alan Draper? Pleased to see the end of your engagement, was she?'

'Pleased, as well as relieved...although she said only three words. *"Told you so."*' Judy admitted with reluctance.

'And your dad? What did he say?'

Judy drew a deep breath. 'All he said was, *"Damned good riddance."*'

'And you? Do you agree with their sentiments? Never mind that tapestry for the moment. Just look at me and tell me the truth.' He took the work from her hands, then drew her to her feet. His eyes gazing into her own had become penetrating, almost as though trying to pierce her mind to learn the state of her emotions.

She nodded vigorously, then had no trouble in meeting his gaze. 'They were perfectly right,' she conceded. 'I'm now wondering how I could've been such a fool.'

'Good,' he said with an air of satisfaction. 'Let's seal that statement with a kiss.'

She went into his arms willingly, and as she responded to the ardour of his lips on her own she knew she was building up heartache for herself. But she brushed the thought aside as the words of a poet flashed into her mind. *'Gather ye rosebuds while ye may.'* These precious moments were like rosebuds that would fade and die the moment Verna arrived to begin family life with Ryan, yet even that thought collapsed beneath the rapture of being held against his body, a body that made no secret of the fact that he wanted to make love.

But suddenly, as on the previous occasion when Ryan had kissed her, Robin's shocked tones dragged them back to earth. 'Uncle Ryan, you're kissing Judy *again*. Is she sad, like the last time?'

'Yes, she is,' Ryan assured him. 'She's in need of tender loving care and a strong man's arms about her. Isn't that so, Judy?' he queried, while looking down into her face.

She knew she had to agree with whatever he said, therefore she nodded wordlessly, feeling unable to speak. And then apprehension gripped her as she whispered to Ryan, 'This will be reported to his grandmother. She'll be livid. She'll have my head on a platter.'

'You leave the dragon to me,' he muttered, then gave her another hug before releasing her.

Next morning spasmodic showers continued to drench the outside scene. Robin, becoming restless, spoke peevishly. 'Uncle Ryan, when is this rain going to stop? I want to go outside.'

Ryan side-stepped the issue. 'Better ask Judy,' he advised. 'She might be able to tell you.'

She joined Robin at the rain-splattered window, then pointed towards the west, where there was a break in the clouds. 'Do you see that patch of blue? Do you think it's large enough to make a pair of pants for a sailor boy?' she said, using the reassurance her mother had always used with her.

Robin spoke morosely. 'I don't know.'

'Well, it is. It means the rain will soon stop,' Judy assured him.

Robin's spirits lifted at once. He sat down at the table and began to eat his breakfast.

As Judy poured her coffee she became aware of Ryan watching her with an intangible expression on his face. She tried to ignore it by cutting Robin's toast into fingers, yet was unable to control the flush that crept into her cheeks. 'Why are you staring at me?' she asked at last.

'I've noticed you have a knack of giving comfort to Robin,' he observed. 'But this time, if the rain doesn't clear, you'll be in trouble. You'll have let him down.'

'I'll deal with that problem when—and if—it comes,' she returned dismissively. Nevertheless, as the morning passed she sent anxious glances towards the sky. To her relief the blue patches widened into large areas, the showers became less, and as soon as lunch was over they went downstairs and crossed the road towards the seafront.

Ryan led them towards a path that crossed the lawn bordering the beach. It took them past the white-fronted two-storey motel into which he had intended putting her when she and Robin had first arrived. Next to the motel was the restaurant, its wide expanse of glass windows revealing people who sat at tables for late lunches.

A short distance beyond the restaurant the path ended when it reached a gravelled parking area. On its far side was a small round tower which housed the gun used for starting the yacht races. And beyond the tower a wave-splashed rocky promontory extended into the sea to mark the channel entrance to the marina and fishing boat harbour.

Robin shouted with glee. 'I'm going to climb over those rocks…'

'No—you must not go near them,' Ryan said sternly.

'I shall! I shall!' Robin yelled defiantly, then raced to-

wards the lengthy mass of jagged boulders, many of which
were draped with slimy wet seaweed.

Ryan caught him before he was past the tower. 'When I
say *no*, I mean *no*,' he roared at the boy. 'Those rocks are
slippery and very dangerous for children. A big wave could
wash you into the sea, so don't you *dare* go near them. Do
you understand?'

Robin looked shaken by Ryan's anger. However, he
didn't fly into one of his usual tantrums, but allowed himself to be led back without further argument.

Judy watched the white foam-crested waves dashing
themselves against the solid walls. She shuddered slightly
as she turned to Ryan and said, 'I'm so thankful you're
here. If Robin and I had made this walk without you I'm
not sure he would have returned so obediently for me. I
might have had trouble with him.'

As though still irritated by Robin's behaviour, he spoke
sharply. 'Is that the only reason you're pleased I'm here?'

She gave a light laugh, then spoke casually. 'I can't
imagine you'd hope there was any other reason.'

'I thought that perhaps you were beginning to find my
company...not too unbearable. Still, it's nice to know I
have my uses.'

She smiled at him. 'You're right on both counts—but
may we leave this place? I wouldn't like that lad to get any
ideas about slipping out of the house and returning alone.'

As they began to make their way along the path Ryan
took Judy's hand. As usual her heart skipped a beat as she
felt his fingers grip her own, but she did not withdraw them.
Instead she tried to give the impression it was no big deal,
and therefore didn't mean a thing to her.

Robin, skipping happily ahead of them, appeared to have
forgotten the rocks. He chased a seagull which landed on
the path leading from the main path to the restaurant door,
and as the bird flew away he stood still to stare at the
building. The next instant he was running towards the glass

doors, where he stood gazing in at the people sitting at tables. A moment later he had disappeared inside.

'What's he up to now?' Ryan gritted impatiently. 'I can see what you mean when you say he has to be watched. He'd send Kate round the bend.'

Robin appeared again almost immediately. He raced towards them, his face flushed and beaming with excitement as he shouted breathlessly, 'Judy! Judy! *He's in there...*'

Judy stood as though rooted to the ground while staring at him. 'Who's in there?' she demanded as he reached her side.

'*Him*...you know...*that man*,' Robin panted. 'Come and see him...'

Ryan frowned. 'Who the devil is he talking about?'

'I've no idea—unless...unless...' She became aware of a growing apprehension that exploded into sudden panic as she went on unsteadily, 'Unless it's Alan Draper. I couldn't bear it if he's followed me here.' She turned to speak to Robin again, but the boy, still on fire with excitement, was already rushing back to the restaurant, where he disappeared through the glass doors.

Ryan made no effort to disguise his curiosity. 'Shall we follow to see what all this is about? If it's Draper I'll tell him to back off...if you're sure that's what you want?'

'Of course I'm sure,' she hissed. 'After what I've told you, how could you doubt it?'

'OK, then come and face up to him.' Ryan took her arm and began to draw her towards the restaurant.

But they had taken only a few steps when the reason for Judy's agitation stepped through the restaurant door. He was accompanied by Robin, who almost danced beside him.

She gave a gasp of amazement as she said with undisguised relief, 'That's not Alan Draper. He's the man who was on the plane...the one who helped me with Robin.'

The man making his way towards them appeared to be in his late thirties. He was casually dressed, in a well-cut brown tweed jacket, worn over a burnt orange polo-neck jersey, and dark brown trousers. He was as tall as Ryan, and, although his dark hair lacked the auburn glint, Judy thought the two men looked surprisingly alike. Or was this because their tanned complexions gave both the appearance of being outdoor men?

The newcomer's dark eyes rested upon Judy with obvious pleasure. 'So we meet again. I could scarcely believe my eyes when I saw the lad staring at me through the glass doors.'

The pink in Judy's cheeks deepened as she said, 'I'm afraid I don't know your name, but I'm Judy Arledge, and this is Ryan Ellison. As for Robin—I think he told you his name on the plane.'

The man laughed, showing good, strong white teeth. 'I think he told everyone on the plane also that he is now six and was going to Napier to stay with Uncle Ryan.' He held out his hand to the latter as he introduced himself. 'Noel Collier. I'm staying at the motel for a few days.'

Judy spoke quickly. 'I'm glad to be able to thank you again for helping me with a certain party on the plane. But how strange that you should be staying so close to where we are.'

Noel said, 'It was necessary for me to come to this area for a little historical research.'

Ryan, who had been subjecting Noel Collier to a close scrutiny, now asked, 'Upon what subject?'

'I need details about a ship known as the *Montmorency*,' Noel explained. 'I've been spending time reading old newspaper cuttings in the museum library. They've been most helpful.'

'Most people round these parts have heard of the *Montmorency*,' Ryan informed him. 'She met her end in these waters by going up in smoke.'

'So I understand.' Noel turned to sweep a glance across the bay. 'That was in 1867. An ancestor of mine was on board. I'm making an effort to put a family history together, and I'd like to include information about the ship.'

Judy spoke anxiously. 'Were any lives lost? Did your ancestor get ashore safely?'

Noel grinned, then said dryly, 'Yes…otherwise I wouldn't be here. It would've been a different matter if the ship had been at sea, but fortunately she was anchored right here in the harbour.'

Judy closed her eyes as a shudder passed through her. 'I can almost imagine flames licking the decks and creeping up the masts while passengers jumped overboard into the sea.'

Noel shook his head. 'In this case there was nothing so dramatic. The fire wasn't discovered until almost midnight, and by that time the passengers and their luggage had been landed. Only the cargo was still intact. I've also learnt that in her day the *Montmorency* was said to have carried more immigrants than any other British ship.'

'Did your ancestor settle in Napier?' Judy had no idea why she was interested in this question.

'Yes, he found work with a blacksmith, because he'd always dealt with horses. Years later the family moved to the Waikato district. I have a farm near Cambridge,' Noel informed them casually.

As Noel spoke Judy became aware of Ryan's watchful attitude. She noticed the olive-green eyes flick from Noel to herself, almost as though assessing her reaction to this newcomer. It caused her to smile inwardly, while recalling his warning about being caught on the rebound.

Noel, she was willing to admit, was a well-built, good-looking man, but he was not to be compared with Ryan. Nor had he been endowed with the latter's charisma that seemed to reach out and touch her. On their first meeting, when she'd thanked Noel for his help with Robin, he had not made her heart thud—whereas Ryan had held an immediate attraction, one she'd been trying to combat ever since. A losing battle, she now admitted to herself, and one which she had almost given in to. In any case, Noel probably had a wife or girlfriend tucked away somewhere.

Noel's voice interrupted her ponderings. 'I was about to order coffee for myself when I saw the lad. Would you care to join me? We might even find an orange drink.'

Ryan looked dubious. 'Actually, we were just on our way home,' he began, with thinly veiled relief. Then, staring upward, he went on, 'That dark cloud looks as if it's about ready to drop its load of rain. We should really keep moving.'

Judy looked at him with surprise. Had he no wish to accept the invitation? It seemed so ungracious, and not at all like Ryan, therefore, as she could see no reason for not doing so, she said, 'It's very kind of you, Mr Collier...'

And then Robin whined plaintively, 'Uncle Ryan—I'm *awful thirsty.*'

But it wasn't Robin's thirst that settled the matter. It was the overhead cloud, which began to send down large spits of rain and caused Ryan to say, 'OK—the restaurant it is.'

As they hurried towards the glass doors Judy pondered upon the strange way in which this man—this Noel Collier—had reappeared on her scene within such a short time. It was almost as though it was part of an event over which she had no control. The sort of thing some people would call fate.

He led them to the window table he'd been occupying when Robin's sharp eyes had first seen him through the glass. A waiter approached and he gave orders for coffee and juice. His voice as he chatted to Ryan was cultured, and as Judy began to observe him more closely she decided that he had a pleasant personality.

Turning to her, Noel spoke quietly. 'It's nice to see you again, especially as you're looking so much less harassed than when you were on the plane. I presume it's because Uncle Ryan is sharing the responsibility of a certain young man.'

Judy smiled ruefully. 'I suppose I did look rather hassled. It's a wonder you've even recognised me.'

There was a pause while Noel's dark eyes lingered on her blonde hair and flawless complexion, then a faint smile touched his lips as he said, 'I'm sure Ryan will agree when I say that your face is somewhat…unforgettable.'

Judy felt the colour rising to her cheeks. The compliment was unexpected, and in the silence that followed she was unable to think of anything to say.

But Robin was not at a loss for words. 'Judy is Uncle Ryan's girlfriend,' he informed Noel. 'He's been *kissing* her. I *saw* him.'

Laughter erupted from the two men, but Judy was not amused. Her face became flooded by a shade of deep crimson, and she felt thoroughly cross with Robin. She also felt hurt by Ryan's laughter, which seemed to confirm that those kisses had meant precisely nothing to him, and, fuming inwardly, she made a silent vow that she would not allow him to kiss her again. But even as she came to this decision she knew she'd be unable to resist the feel of his lips on her own, or the joy of his arms holding her against his body.

But at least the laughter had eased the tension that seemed to have descended upon Ryan, Judy noticed, while trying to discern the reason for the grim lines that had been hovering about his mouth. Was he annoyed because Noel had paid her a compliment? No…of course not. She was being ridiculous. Ryan couldn't care less about a few kind words being tossed in her direction. In any case, what right had he to object to another man saying her face was unforgettable? Anyone would imagine he was jealous. Now *that* was something to laugh about.

Impulsively, an imp of defiance forced her to centre her attention on Noel, and, as though really interested, she said, 'Please tell us about your farm. Do you graze sheep or cattle?'

He grinned boyishly, giving the impression that his farm

was something he really enjoyed talking about. 'I have both sheep and cattle…and I breed ponies for children.'

Robin became alert, staring at him wide-eyed. '*Ponies*…you've got *ponies*? Please…may I call you Uncle Noel?'

'I'd be honoured, old chap,' Noel said over the chuckles Robin's plea had caused.

'We're rather pony-conscious at the moment,' Ryan explained dryly. 'We've just had our first donkey ride, which didn't come up to expectations because Neddy has given up galloping—'

'So Uncle Ryan is taking me to a pony club,' Robin cut in.

Noel displayed more interest than expected. 'Would you mind telling me where and when it's to be held? I have a rental car and I'd like to see a few ponies while I'm in this area. I'm always on the look-out for good new stock.'

There was a silence before Ryan spoke gruffly. 'There's no need to find your own way there. If it's any help, come with us tomorrow in the Range Rover.'

'Thank you…I'd like that.' Noel spoke quietly.

Judy felt glad the invitation had been issued. She had sensed Ryan's previous animosity towards Noel, and could only hope it had now disappeared. Turning to the latter, she said, 'Is your farm a family property?'

Ryan frowned, while sending her a strange glance, then he said to Noel, 'You'll have to excuse a bad case of female curiosity.'

A flush touched Judy's cheeks. 'I'm not prying,' she said defensively. 'I merely wondered if Noel had brothers to take over while he's absent.'

'That's OK,' Noel said placatingly. 'But, no…it has never been what could be called a family farm. It had always belonged to my father, who was so possessive he'd never allow me to have any say in the running of the place. And I was his only child…'

'Why didn't you branch out and find a job elsewhere?' Ryan queried.

'I did, for a short time. Then, after my mother's death, he became ill and I had to return home. I can tell you the house was not an easy place to live in,' Noel said grimly, then he sighed and went on, 'I inherited the property after his death, which took place several months ago. However, probate has now been granted and the farm belongs to me. The men my father employed are still with me. They enable me to get away for the odd break.'

'Like taking a trip to Christchurch,' Judy said with a smile. 'Robin told us that you know his little friend, Sally.'

'Yes—it's a small world. Sally is my cousin Wendy's child. Wendy's mother and my mother were sisters. It's a few years since I was able to visit them.'

Ryan stood up with a definite air of assuming control. 'The rain has stopped,' he declared with decision. 'We'll leave now, before it comes on again.'

Judy realised he was calling the tune, but she made no objection. She merely turned to Noel and said, 'I'm sure Ryan will let you know what time we're going to the pony club.'

He had risen to his feet. 'I look forward to it,' he said, in a voice that echoed sincerity.

Ryan held the door open for her, and as they walked along the path a tense silence lay between them, until his voice came harshly. 'So…he's looking forward to seeing you again soon.'

'He didn't say that,' Judy retorted swiftly.

'It's what he meant.'

'Nonsense. He's just looking forward to going to the *pony club*. I'm sure *that's* what he meant.'

'Well, you could've fooled me,' Ryan flung over his shoulder, while striding along with Robin running beside him.

Judy had to hasten to keep up with them. Ryan's hands, she noticed, were kept stuffed in his pockets. She couldn't help wondering if she was being given a message. Holding her hand before had been a mistake. The fact that he was displeased was obvious, yet she was unable to pin down the cause.

When they reached home Robin settled down with his bricks while Ryan disappeared downstairs to his office and shut the door. It was further proof of his anger, Judy thought as she combed her wind-blown hair before the dressing-table mirror. A nervous tension gripped her, and to give herself more confidence she applied an extra touch of make-up. She also changed from her trouser suit into one of the few feminine dresses she had brought, then, just as she was about to leave the bedroom, Ryan appeared in the doorway.

For a moment she just stared at his tightened jawline, then courage enabled her to say, 'I know something's niggling at you...so why don't you get it off your chest?'

'I've come to do just that.' The words were clipped. 'I'd like to know when you intend to see him again. I take it an arrangement has been made?'

She was astounded by the accusation. 'You mean...with Noel?'

He spoke ironically. 'Who else could I have in mind? Who else has been bringing colour to your face during the last couple of hours? Those big blue eyes positively shine.'

Taken aback, she faced him indignantly. 'What are you talking about?'

'As if you don't know,' he scoffed.

Bewildered, she queried, in a voice that was not quite steady, 'When did I make the...this supposed "arrangement"? Weren't you with us all the time?'

'Not when I went to get more coffee,' he pointed out grimly. 'It could've happened then, in a subtle manner, over Robin's head.'

'How can you be so suspicious of me?' she flared at him, at the same time making an effort to hide the hurt his words had caused.

He shrugged. 'Years ago I learnt that women are not to be trusted. It's one of the reasons I've kept them out of my home.' He hesitated, then went on, 'Personally, I think the compliment Collier paid you went to your head. It stirred your interest in him and made you ask questions about his farm and background.'

'For heaven's sake, I was only trying to be polite,' she protested in dismay, exasperation making her voice shake.

His face darkened as his tone became sardonic. 'I was waiting for you to ask if his wife keeps good health.'

Puzzled, she blinked at him. 'Good health...?'

'It would've told you whether he's married or not,' he mocked.

Her chin rose as she hissed, 'His marital status is of no interest to me, and you've no right to suggest it. What *does* concern me is that he was very helpful on the plane and I'll not forget it.'

'What he did was no big deal,' he growled.

'It meant a lot to me,' she snapped. 'If I'd tried to force Robin into his seat I could've had a tantrum on my hands. I can tell you—Noel Collier was a godsend.'

'Yes, I suppose you're right,' Ryan conceded, after pausing moodily, 'Young Robin needs a man about the place. He needs to be taught discipline.'

'Preferably from his *father*,' Judy said pointedly, at the same time subjecting Ryan to a direct stare that held accusation. 'It's a pity his *father* couldn't see fit to share the responsibility of the boy. The older he gets, the more difficult he'll become.'

'I couldn't agree more,' Ryan admitted.

'OK, so if you can understand my problem on the plane, why are you so cross because I showed a polite interest in Noel's farm?' she demanded, as though pushing home an advantage.

Frowning at her in silence, he appeared to be searching for an answer. Then, taking a few steps closer, he stared down into her face. 'Possibly it's because I suspect you haven't given a second thought to my warning,' he rasped.

'Your…your warning?' She gaped at him uncomprehendingly.

'You *see*—you *have* forgotten. It was about being caught on the rebound,' he reminded her triumphantly.

'Oh—that!' She gave a small shaky laugh.

'Yes—*that*,' he gritted. 'You've deliberately ignored my advice.'

She stared at him incredulously. 'You're saying your reason for being so mad with me is because I didn't follow your advice? Well, for your information—I don't believe you. I mean…I don't believe that was your *real* reason.'

His eyes became hooded as he growled, 'At the moment it's as good as any other reason. As for further discussion, the subject is closed. Is that understood?'

'Very well—but any fool can see you're being evasive,' she flung at him, then turned away to hide the piercing hurt growing steadily within her. His refusal to be frank seemed to have raised a brick wall between them, and pride would not allow her to climb over it.

A prickling behind her lids caused her to move towards the window, where she stared unseeingly through the wet pane. Outside the rain was falling again, the damp greyness of the day reflecting her own low spirits. She swallowed, trying to steady her voice, then said, 'I had been hoping there could be honesty between us—but it seems as if…as if—' She broke off, unable to go on.

Ryan crossed the room to stand beside her. 'You're right,' he declared. 'Honesty between us is essential.'

Miserably she thought, Then why haven't you admitted to being Robin's father?

But apparently his thoughts were not with the boy, and he surprised her by saying, 'You're also right about there being another reason for my black mood, but now is not the time to air something that's purely personal.'

'I've no wish to pry,' she murmured shakily, then felt

herself go tense as his hands turned her to face him. The firm pressure of his fingers caused her breath to quicken, then sent a tremor through her. It was like being under a hypnotic spell that prevented her from dragging her eyes from the intensity of his olive-green gaze. Strangely, she sensed him to be aware of an emotion that appeared to displease him. His jaw tightened until a muscle worked in his cheek, then, unexpectedly, he relaxed and lowered his head.

His lips trailed across her forehead before touching her lids with butterfly softness. Her cheeks, now crimson, came in for gentle caresses. *Could he hear the pounding of her heart?* she wondered. Did he know the blood was rushing through her veins like molten lava? It was only when his mouth found hers that she stopped asking herself questions and melted against him.

She was revelling in the feel of his arms crushing her against his body, and ecstasy caused her eyes to close. As the kiss deepened with lingering sensuality throbs of desire vibrated through every nerve, making her long to be held even closer, and for the kiss to go on for ever.

But it did not. A shuddering sigh shook him as his lips left hers, and then Judy felt herself being put from him in a firm but gentle manner. Her eyes flew open and she looked at him with bewilderment. For a few moments she'd been floating heavenwards, but now that her feet were back on the ground she felt confused. 'I'd...I'd better go and see what we can have for dinner this evening,' she stammered.

'You do that,' he said in a low, husky voice. 'Personally, I'll go and have a cold shower—otherwise I'll carry you to that bed. It's very close and very tempting. Do you understand?'

She nodded wordlessly. Oh, yes, she understood. Hadn't she just been vitally aware of his arousal? She fled to the kitchen.

CHAPTER SIX

JUDY'S heart continued to flutter like a trapped bird, and as she stared at the contents of the fridge she hardly knew what she was looking for. Ryan wanted her, she knew it for a certainty, but common sense warned that it was only because of male sexual hunger, and the thought was a sobering one. It caused her to take several deep breaths, pull herself together and drag her mind down from where it seemed to be floating. It also enabled her to decide upon a meal and to set about preparing it.

Later, when Robin was in bed and the dishwasher was coping with that particular chore, Judy again found herself gripped by an inner excitement she found hard to control. It was fuelled by anticipation. Would Ryan kiss her again this evening? She yearned for him to do so, but kept her longing well hidden by showing a casual front as she sat curled on the settee with a magazine.

However, although she flicked the odd look in his direction, she soon became aware that Ryan sent scarcely a glance towards her. His well-muscled legs stretched before him, his athletic body relaxed in an armchair, he appeared to have become immersed in the local newspaper. Hidden behind it, he was obviously reading every word in every column, and apart from the occasional rustle as he turned a page, the silence in the room became difficult for Judy's nerves to bear.

It caused her frustration to reach simmering point, and it was only with an effort that she forced herself to remain calm and to accept the fact that Ryan had no intention of kissing her again that evening. As for coming to her room—that was the last thing he had in mind. Not that she

93

was *really* hoping for that, she tried to assure herself crossly. Wasn't she the person who, until recently, had sworn to remain unattached?

Even so, when she climbed between the sheets she lay tense and wide-eyed while listening for the sound of his movements, until at last she chided herself for being a fool. Restlessly, she turned over and thumped the pillow as the voice of common sense whispered in her mind. Go to sleep, you idiot, it said. Can't you see that kisses from Ryan will develop into a very flimsy affair that'll last for only as long as you're here? When the time for departure comes he'll kiss you goodbye and *that will be that*. You'll never hear from him again. He knows that, and you'd be wise to wake up to it as well. So don't lie listening for his footsteps because they won't come.

On this point common sense was right. They didn't.

When Judy woke next morning she felt herself to be in a clearer state of mind—at least clear enough to feel annoyed with herself for having allowed those moments of closeness with Ryan to affect her so strongly. Sleep, when it had come, had been deep and refreshing, and, she assured herself, had swept all thoughts of romance from her mind. She was back to her normal self. She'd be able to look Ryan in the eye without her silly heart tripping over itself whenever he came near.

And this proved to be easier than expected, because Ryan's attitude towards her was so casual she doubted that he even remembered that he'd held her in his arms. So be it, she told herself with a resigned sigh, then set about looking out the clothes Robin would wear when they went to the pony club. His warm jacket, she noticed, needed a small repair, but a sewing kit was something she'd neglected to bring with her, and the embroidery needles just wouldn't do.

To Ryan she said, 'I don't suppose there are such items as needle and thread in this house?'

An amused glint crept into his eyes. 'Why would you assume that this house should be so deprived?'

'Only because I would expect Kate to do all your repair jobs.'

He grinned. 'You're mistaken. I'm a most versatile man. I can sew on a button.'

She looked at the bulge of chest and arm muscles beneath his green jersey, then a laugh escaped her as she said, 'The thought of your long fingers manipulating a fine needle is something I find difficult to imagine.'

'Well, it doesn't happen too often,' he admitted. 'And you're right about Kate attending to garments that need repair. She simply gets rid of them, but don't ask me where they go.' He paused, then raised one brow. 'Why this wish for a needle and thread?'

'Dark thread, if possible, please. The stitching holding the zip of Robin's jacket has become broken. I'd like to mend it before it goes any further and leaves his front gaping open.' She left him and went to fetch the jacket from the bedroom the small boy was occupying.

Ryan examined it. 'He's likely to pull the threads and make it worse. That's also the trouble with a button. Pull a thread and it drops off.'

'That's because it hasn't been sewn on securely in the first place.' Another giggle escaped her.

He scowled. 'What's so funny?'

'The thought of you...sewing on a button.'

'Really amusing, is it? You wouldn't be hinting I need a woman in the house, I suppose? I mean—permanently.'

'Of course not, especially when Kate is next door to attend to such matters,' she said hastily, then was unable to resist adding, 'Although I doubt that she gives you much company.'

'You're suggesting I'm in need of company?'

Before she could answer he strode from the room, and moments later returned with a box containing light and dark cottons, needles and a pair of scissors. He then sat and watched while she made short work of the small repair job, and as she snipped the cotton he pursued, 'What makes you so sure I'm in need of company?'

The suggestion had niggled at him, she realised, and, choosing her words carefully, she said, 'There must be times when you're lonely...especially in the evenings.'

A snort echoed faintly. 'You're picturing a poor, miserable fellow who's alone each night? Believe me, most of the time there aren't enough hours in which to do everything I've planned. I'm not normally sitting about in this manner.'

Her voice low, she said, 'No, I suppose not. I was forgetting you're on vacation—one that's been thrown out of gear by the arrival of Robin and myself.'

'It might surprise you to learn I wouldn't have had it otherwise,' he informed her with an enigmatic smile.

Her eyes widened. 'Surprise me? It *amazes* me—and it's very kind of you to say so, but I understand it's because it has enabled you to see and spend time with Robin. I suppose you'll miss him when he leaves.'

'You think so?' His smile had vanished, and there were now grim lines about his mouth, a sure sign that she'd angered him.

The sight of them made her feel that a different topic would be tactful, and, searching in her mind for one that would feature his interests, she said, 'Tell me about your usual day. I mean the type of day you have when you're not on vacation.'

He contemplated her thoughtfully. 'It would really interest you?'

'Of course, otherwise I wouldn't ask.'

He frowned momentarily as he said, 'I doubt that any of my days can be termed "usual". They're all quite varied, although you can rely on them being spent with the men. I'm not a boss who sits in a cosy office while shouting orders over a phone. Come hail or shine I'm out working with them, moving from one block to another, depending upon the season and what's going on at the time.'

She recalled the welcome the men had given Ryan when he'd arrived at the apple orchard and at the vineyard, but all she said was, 'No wonder you look so tanned and fit and well. Where does it all start?'

'You mean the work? It begins with the preparing of the ground,' he informed her. 'Haven't you heard that for everything there is a season?'

'Like a time to sow and a time to reap?'

'There's also a time to fertilise the land, which becomes hungry and has to be fed. There's a time to prune and a time to spray to protect the crops. Later there's harvesting. There's not much joy in having a good crop if you can't get it harvested. And those are only a few of the daytime jobs,' he pointed out.

She looked at him wonderingly. 'There are also *evening* jobs?'

'That's when I'm in the office, attending to paperwork. Accounts must be paid, seeds have to be ordered, along with other necessities for the various blocks. There's more to it than you think. Sure you're not becoming bored?' he queried softly.

'Not even remotely. Please tell me more,' she pleaded, finding it impossible to hide her eagerness.

After that she listened avidly while he continued to talk about the development of the different crops under cultivation each year. And as he spoke of the numerous problems that could arise she knew she was learning more about him. He was a quietly determined man, she realised. He was one who achieved his goals without fuss. Had he learnt patience through dealing with nature and having to wait for crops to ripen? A season for everything, he'd said.

When she left this place she'd remember those words. They'd help to prevent him from becoming a remote or shadowy figure. They'd enable her to visualise him in the orchard or the vineyard, or maybe just out in a large area of recently ploughed land.

His voice came through the maze of her thoughts, startling her with its abrupt change of subject. 'By the way, Cynthia phoned. She's tracked down a grey pony mare that's for sale. Apparently the owner has outgrown her and is now going to boarding-school. Collier might be interested in her. Named Bluebell, I believe.'

'That's a nice name. I hope she'll be suitable.' A smile lit Judy's face as she went on, 'Just imagine having lots of lovely little ponies about the place. Noel's farm must be a children's paradise.'

He sent her a sharp glance. 'So, Collier has children?'

'I didn't say that. I've really no idea about what he has…'

Ryan's eyes held a piercing glint. 'And you still don't yet know whether he's married or a free agent?'

Judy was startled by the question. 'I certainly wouldn't ask,' she protested. 'And he hasn't mentioned a wife… or…or a partner of any description.'

Ryan shrugged. 'Well, that's not surprising. Some men like to keep these matters a dead secret—especially when they're away from home and in another district. Show them a pretty face and they fail to admit they have a wife—'

'While some men fail to admit they have a child,' Judy cut in, the words slipping out before she could stop them.

Ryan's eyes narrowed. 'What the hell's that supposed to mean?' he demanded ominously, his mouth becoming grim again.

'What it says—that some men refuse to stand by their offspring. I know of one little boy who could do with his father standing beside him,' she said pointedly, at the same time wondering where she'd found the courage to utter these words.

'I presume you're referring to Robin. Where is he?'

'In his room, reading,' she told him, while watching a small muscle work in his cheek. Then she went on boldly,

'Now that he's at school he'll see other boys with fathers. He's sure to ask questions—but heaven alone knows what Verna will tell him.'

'Is it possible you're hinting that *I* should do something about this situation?' he gritted in a low tone.

'Well…surely it's up to you to do the right thing by the boy,' she said serenely, while becoming conscious of an inner satisfaction. There now—that should tell him I've guessed he's Robin's father, she thought, then waited for him to either admit or deny it.

He did neither. Instead, his expression became glacial, his jaw tightening as he rasped, 'Then hear this: Robin's situation is one I refuse to discuss. Is that understood?'

Inwardly her satisfaction switched almost to fear as she quailed beneath his anger, but she returned his cold glare steadily as she said, 'I can see it's useless to even try.'

'Good. Then that fixes that.' His tone changed to one of cynicism. 'Personally, I consider it much more to the point for you to start wondering about Collier's marital status before you lap up too many of his compliments. They might go to your head. They might even cause you to do something stupid.'

'Like what?' she snapped.

'Like following him home to pat his ponies!' Ryan sneered cynically.

'I'm unlikely to do that,' she retorted indignantly, then, staring at him through troubled eyes, she went on, 'He seems to be such a nice man, yet you're beginning to sound as though you don't like him. What have you got against him?'

Ryan frowned thoughtfully. 'To be honest, I don't know. There's something about him that bothers me…something I'm unable to put my finger on. Women may have intuition, but men also have an instinct, you know. Has he made a pass at you?' The question came fiercely.

'No…you know he hasn't…but if you're feeling antagonistic towards him why did you say he could come to the pony club with us?'

'I've no idea. In some smooth way he seems to have infiltrated himself into our company. Yesterday I'd never even heard of him. Today I'll be running him about the countryside.' Ryan sounded aggrieved. He moved restlessly, and it was obvious the situation annoyed him.

Judy smiled. 'I'm sure you're worrying needlessly,' she said. 'You'll find he just wants to learn if there's a pony for sale—one that's not related to any of his own stock. In any case, he gave me the impression he'll be leaving within the next few days.'

Was it her imagination, or did Ryan actually give a sigh of relief? Watching him, she tried to fathom what he could have against a pleasant personality like Noel Collier. Surely he couldn't be *jealous* because Noel had offered herself a few kind words. Or was he afraid of the effect Noel might have on Cynthia? And in that case just how deep were his own feelings for Cynthia?

Forget it...forget it... she cried silently within herself, and in an effort to clear her mind she went to the kitchen and opened the fridge door. 'We're almost out of milk. We should go to the supermarket,' she said in a matter-of-fact voice.

Ryan came to the kitchen. 'We also need tonic water and crisps, otherwise we'll be deprived of our relaxing G and T at the sunset hour. You'd better make a list.'

She wrote rapidly, using the pen and pad kept beside the phone on the worktop, the task helping to settle her previous unruly thoughts back to a more even keel.

As the list of items grew Ryan moved closer, then placed his arm across her shoulders while reading it. 'I appear to have been neglecting the shopping,' he admitted ruefully. 'Maybe a woman in the house makes all the difference to the running of it.'

She revelled in the feel of his touch, which sent quivers down her spine, but his words forced her to straighten her

back and turn to gaze at him in wide-eyed amazement.
'Now I've heard *everything*,' she said. '*That*—coming from
you—is the statement of the year.'

'What do you mean?' he growled.

She giggled. 'I recall meeting a man who was determined
to *keep women out of his house*. Strangely, he looked just
like you.'

His mouth twisted into a hard line. 'Did he, indeed?
Have you forgotten he has a damned good reason for it?'
His voice had cooled.

'No, I haven't forgotten,' she returned quietly. 'I merely
presumed you'd got over that particular episode. But there's
no need for you to worry. When I leave here you'll soon
be back to normal. Within a short time you'll forget that a
woman ever darkened your doorway.' Her words dwindled
to a whisper, leaving a sharp pain hovering just below her
throat.

'When you leave here…?' he repeated in a low voice,
his face completely unreadable although his eyes seemed
to have darkened.

'That's right,' she said, with a forced brightness she was
far from feeling. 'I'll soon be out of your hair. The days
are passing and the school holidays will soon be over.'
Hesitantly, she added, 'No doubt you'll miss the boy…'

'But not yourself. Is that what you're trying to say?'

'I won't be expecting you to miss me—especially when
I'm so good at saying things that make you mad,' she admitted ruefully.

'Then why say them?'

'I don't mean to annoy you,' she tried to explain. 'I'm
only trying to help the boy. Can't you understand that? It's
so sad to see him without a father who will acknowledge
him…and…and I really believe *that's* why his grandmother sent him here.' She was silenced by the look on his
face, and by a sudden feeling that she was out of her depth.
But at least she'd driven the point home.

'I can see you've got it all worked out,' Ryan gritted,

his tight lips betraying an anger that seemed ready to erupt. But before it could burst forth Robin came into the room.

The little boy looked up at him beseechingly. 'When are we going to the pony club? Can we go *now*?'

Ryan's anger appeared to have evaporated. He ruffled the boy's hair and said, 'Not until after lunch, old chap. First we must buy food or we'll all be hungry.'

Judy was glad of the interruption. Ryan's anger, she'd noticed, was soon over. Nor did he appear to sulk, and because she was thankful for these facts she lifted Robin on to a kitchen stool and gave him a hug.

Ryan watched Judy's affection towards the boy, and as the hug ended he queried, 'Now can we go to the supermarket?'

Noticing the amused look on his face, she felt slightly disconcerted. 'Something makes you want to laugh?' she demanded.

'Nothing at all.' He spoke smoothly, his eyes becoming hooded.

But she was not convinced, and as she hurried along the passage to collect her blue jacket she wondered if he thought her attentions to Robin had been a ploy to impress him. Once before he'd made a similar accusation, she recalled. On that occasion it had made her angry, but this time was different. This time it hurt.

She made a silent vow to keep off the subject of Robin's father. It would have been nice to have discussed the situation in a normal manner, but obviously Ryan had no wish to do this. The mere mention of it seemed to drive him up the wall, and she could see that if she persisted her remaining days with him could become most unpleasant. Why was he so touchy about it? she wondered. Was it because of guilt? Yet guilt was something she found impossible to associate with Ryan.

A short time later she was feeling more cheerful as they walked between the rows of stacked shelves in the supermarket. Ryan pushed the trolley—with Robin's help—

while Judy consulted the list and placed their purchases in it. Never before had she shopped with a man, and suddenly she found herself enjoying the experience which, in a strange way, gave her a feeling of deep satisfaction.

It also gave her an intangible feeling of belonging to the man at her side. There was an intimacy about it that filled her with contentment, especially when their heads or hands almost touched when they bent over the list. It was then that she became aware of the fragrance of his aftershave, and the fresh, male cleanliness that tantalised her nostrils. What was the matter with her? she wondered. This was just an ordinary shopping expedition—wasn't it? Instinctively she knew it was more than that. It was something to be remembered when she left this place.

She was still in a euphoric daze when they reached home, and this pleasurable state of mind caused her to hum the chorus of a popular song while placing a previously pre-pared lunch in the microwave oven.

Ryan's ear caught the subdued melody. 'You sound as if you're happy,' he remarked. 'Does this mean you're looking forward to this afternoon?' The olive-green eyes glinted while watching her closely.

The song died on her lips as she tried to think quickly. It was impossible to tell him the truth, or to admit that his company was beginning to mean something to her. Then a flash of inspiration made her say, 'Yes—a drive out into the country will be lovely…especially when there's sun-shine in winter.'

He sent her a mirthless grin. 'Is that your *real* reason? Don't you mean especially when Noel Collier will be pres-ent?'

She turned to stare at him in surprise. 'I can't believe that such a thought would concern you,' she said. 'One would almost imagine…' She stopped before the accusa-tion of jealousy slipped out. To suggest she thought he could be jealous would certainly give him a laugh.

'Yes? One would almost imagine…what?' he queried softly.

'That you don't realise you're constantly *cross* with me. At least Noel won't make me feel I have to watch every word I say.' Then she brushed the subject aside by removing the dish from the microwave. 'Come and eat this before it goes cold,' she advised, while carrying it towards the table.

During lunch Judy sensed that something continued to niggle at Ryan. He appeared to have little to say, and at times a scowl marred his handsome features. In an effort to break one of his long silences, she said, 'You're very quiet, Ryan. Is there something wrong with your lunch? It's only macaroni cheese with bits of bacon and tomato tossed into it.'

He spoke gravely. 'It's very tasty. You're a good cook. I'll miss you when you're not here.'

When you're not here. The words seemed to stab at her, yet the inward hurt was covered by an outward appearance of cheerfulness. 'What you really mean is when I'm not here to place food before you,' she said teasingly.

'Is that what you think? Well, so be it,' he returned morosely.

He's in a black mood, she realised, then decided it had been caused by her own remarks concerning his responsibility towards Robin. Well—it had been good to get them off her chest—and too bad if they'd maddened him. It was Robin who mattered most.

Despite Ryan's gloom at the table, Judy tried to keep her own spirits buoyant. The morning had held joy for her, and she had no intention of allowing this pleasant feeling to slip away—and, although she knew that Ryan watched her through narrowed lids, she could only guess at his thoughts. However, they were revealed when they were about to leave for the pony club.

'I can see you're up in the air,' Ryan said in a sardonic

tone. 'Would you prefer Robin to sit beside me so that you and Collier can chat more easily?'

She was shocked by the suggestion. 'Certainly not. Noel is your guest. He'll sit in front beside you.'

'OK—if that is your wish.'

'It's *definitely* my wish,' she retorted.

Later, as they drove over the mountainous road towards Te Pohue, Judy was relieved to hear the two men talking amicably. And as she listened to their conversation she could hear that it centred upon the land and what it would produce. A subject of mutual interest, she realised.

She was also thankful to note that Ryan appeared to have lost his previous dark moodiness, and was now acting as an affable host towards Noel. And, although she listened for any probing to learn the latter's marital status, there was not the slightest hint of it.

A short distance before Te Pohue they turned off the twisting highway to follow a gravelled back country road. It led them towards a wide area of flat land, and a few minutes later they came to a large field where the pony club was being held. Ryan turned in at an open gateway and parked beside a number of vehicles with horse-trailers attached to their tow-bars.

The extensive grassy area appeared to be occupied by adults, teenagers, children and ponies—the latter in a variety of sizes. Several young riders were taking their mounts over low hurdles, while others were being instructed in dressage. People stood chatting, and as Judy got out of the Range Rover she saw Cynthia detach herself from a group and come towards them. She was leading a grey pony.

As Noel was introduced to her he spoke with gratitude. 'It was kind of you to find a pony, especially one that's for sale.'

'Oh, I did it for Robin,' Cynthia began virtuously.

But Noel wasn't listening. His attention had become riveted on the pony. With the air of an expert he scrutinised Bluebell's teeth, eyes and feet, then ran practised hands along her neck, over her body and down each leg. At last he spoke to Robin. 'OK, lad—let's see how she behaves.' He lifted the boy on to the sheepskin strapped to the pony's back. 'Head up and grip with your knees,' he said, then led the pony away from the club's activities and towards the fenceline surrounding the field.

Judy stood watching them go. Robin's shining face indicated his sheer delight, and she felt so happy for him. His first ride on a real pony—it had to be the highlight of his visit to Uncle Ryan.

And then Ryan's voice hit her ears like a dash of cold water. 'Why don't you go with them?' he queried in a faintly mocking tone.

She swung round to stare at him, her spirits sinking. 'Robin doesn't need me at present,' she said. 'He'll be all right with Noel—unless...unless you're telling me to go...?'

He said, 'If you've a secret yearning to know Collier better—now is your great opportunity.'

The sardonic ring in his voice riled her, and, feeling frustrated, she repeated the question. 'I'm asking you again— are you telling me to go?'

'I had no wish to put it so blatantly,' he drawled, 'but, yes—I am telling you to go. Cynthia has a financial problem she wishes to discuss. It concerns one of her investments, so naturally it's a private matter. I hope you'll understand.'

Was this true? Or was it that he wished to be alone with Cynthia? she wondered. Regarding him steadily, her chin held slightly higher, she said, 'Of course I understand. I was forgetting you're her minder.'

Cynthia's triumphant laugh rang on the air. '*Minder?* For heaven's sake, Judy, haven't you realised he's much more to me than that?' She turned a rapturous face to Ryan. 'Aren't you, *darling?*'

Judy did not wait to hear Ryan's reply. She turned blindly and began to walk across the field to join Noel and

Robin, who were now a distance away. Her eyes had filled with tears, her blurred vision causing her to stumble in places where the ground was uneven, but she kept going while dabbing at her eyes, blowing her nose and making an effort to get her emotions under control.

Idiot, she fumed with self-derision. So much for walking on air this morning. Now it's afternoon and your feet are back on the ground with a vengeance. Let that teach you not to be carried away by stupid wishful thinking.

Noel glanced over his shoulder as she reached them. 'Two's company, three's a crowd?' he queried ironically.

'That's it exactly,' she returned brightly, and as though she couldn't care less.

His dark brows rose as he regarded her quizzically. 'But I thought you and Ryan…or was I mistaken about that?'

'You were quite mistaken. That was only Robin's idea.' Judy uttered the words with a carefree laugh. At least she hoped it sounded carefree, because inside she was feeling hollow and miserable. Then she drew a deep breath and changed the subject. 'So, what do you think of Bluebell? To me she looks like every child's dream.'

Noel smiled knowingly. 'Most ponies look like children's dreams on the outside. It's their inner vices you have to discover.'

They went round the edge of the large field several times, and as they followed the fenceline Noel told Judy about various ponies he'd had on his farm. When she questioned him further about Bluebell he admitted he was impressed by her—in fact sufficiently impressed to wish to learn more details, such as her exact age and the price being asked for her.

Eventually the pony ride came to an end. Bluebell was returned to the club organiser, who gave Noel all the information he required. After that, with Robin skipping ahead, they made their way back to the Range Rover.

Secretly, Judy had been grateful for the extra time taken up by Noel's talk with the organiser. It had delayed their return to the company of Ryan and Cynthia, which was something she'd been dreading. Was she now to be subjected to the sight of amorous glances slipping between them? The thought was so intolerable it caused depression to settle upon her.

However, when they reached the vehicle she found she had little to fear. Ryan's attitude towards Cynthia appeared to be one of patient amusement, while the latter's plan was for Noel to see Neddy.

Turning her charm upon him, she said, 'Ryan tells me you have a farm. I'm wondering if you could find a corner on it for a nice little donkey. Of course he'd be a gift.'

Noel spoke abruptly. 'I don't accept gifts of livestock. There's usually something wrong with the animal.'

'There's nothing wrong with Neddy,' Cynthia exclaimed indignantly. Then she went on in a pleading tone, 'You see, I *must* find a home for him. Ryan thinks I should move to live in Napier, and I can't leave poor Neddy to fend for himself.'

Noel looked at her thoughtfully. 'Well, I can at least look at him,' he said, without committing himself.

Judy hardly heard Noel's reply because Cynthia's words had begun to swim in her mind. Had Ryan really said she *should* live in Napier? Even Judy herself could see the advantages for Cynthia to do so, but the point was—did Ryan *want* her to live in Napier?

No doubt he would have told Cynthia that Noel had a farm. Perhaps he'd even suggested that if Noel gave Neddy a home she'd be able to make the move. Obviously Cynthia's finances hadn't been the only subject under discussion while the pony ride had been taking place.

Judy also recalled that Ryan had not been over-keen to bring Noel to Te Pohue. But, despite his vague antagonism towards the man, he had brought him, and now she began to wonder why. Had a home for Neddy been the main objective? The thought made her feel miserable.

A short time later they were sitting round Cynthia's

kitchen table. Tea had been made, orange juice produced for Robin, and fingers of homemade shortbread set out on a plate.

Noel drained his cup in an unhurried manner, then stood up. 'OK, so where is this donkey?' he queried.

Cynthia led him outside with an eagerness she was unable to conceal. Robin scrambled down from the table and ran after them through the back door, his mouth still full of shortbread.

Judy remained seated. She looked at Ryan, who had not moved. 'Aren't you going out to learn the verdict?' she asked, while trying to hide the depression that now gripped her. 'Naturally you're aware of what all this is about?'

'I'd have to be mighty dumb to be *unaware* of it.' He grinned.

Extreme irritation began to loosen her tongue, causing pent-up feelings to spill out. 'It's easy to guess that this was your real reason for bringing Noel to Te Pohue,' she said. 'It wasn't to help him find a *pony*—it was to help him find a *donkey*.' Her blue eyes became shadowed as she went on in a low voice that held accusation, 'Matters of finance to be discussed, you said—but this is what you really wanted to talk about...the getting rid of Neddy—' She stopped suddenly, appalled by what she was saying. *Shut up, you fool,* she stormed inwardly at herself. You have no right—nor is it your business.

Ryan glared at her in angry surprise. 'You're jumping to conclusions,' he gritted harshly through tight lips. 'For your information we discussed a share offer, and after that Cynthia wanted to know about Collier and where we'd met him.'

Judy bit her lip. She knew she'd been idiotic to allow her emotions to run away with her, and the embarrassment of it was making her feel mortified. 'I'm sorry, I don't know what got into me,' she mumbled contritely.

Ignoring the apology, Ryan went on in a clipped tone. 'During the drive here Collier told me a little about his farm. Apparently he has a couple of hundred hectares. When I mentioned this to Cynthia she immediately saw a home for Neddy. It'll be good if Collier agrees to take him.'

'It will?' Judy's spirits plummeted to zero. 'Does that mean you'll allow Cynthia to move in with you? But of course—didn't I hear you admit that a woman in the house makes a difference?'

Ryan looked at her with a sardonic glint in his eyes, but before he could reply the others came in. He turned to Noel expectantly. 'Well? Are you taking him?'

Noel was non-committal. 'I don't know. I haven't made up my mind. I'll have to think about it.'

'OK, you do that. Now then, it's time we weren't here. Into the Range Rover, please.' His orders for departure became brisk, and within minutes they were winding their way over the hills.

CHAPTER SEVEN

Judy was more than thankful to be making the journey home. Her pent up emotions were causing her to feel drained, but she endeavoured to keep a bright face while listening to the conversation of the two men sitting in front.

Secretly, she hoped that Noel might reveal his thoughts concerning Neddy, but this did not happen. Nor did Ryan give the slightest hint that he was interested in Noel's decision. Instead he chatted about the early history of this particular highway, telling how it had begun as a Maori track leading from Lake Taupo to Napier, and had later been developed into a road by the Military Forces of the day.

Judy found herself becoming more frustrated than interested. And, while she loved listening to Ryan's deep voice, she didn't want to hear about the early Maori troubles of the district—at least not at that moment. She wanted to know what Noel felt about Neddy. A smile touched her soft lips as she realised that never before had she known of a situation which depended so much on a donkey!

When they arrived at the motel she roused Robin, who had been dozing beside her. 'Wake up, dear, we're almost home. You must say goodnight to Uncle Noel—and I don't think I've heard you thank him for the wonderful ride he gave you on Bluebell.'

'Thank you, Uncle Noel,' Robin murmured sleepily.

'It was a pleasure, lad,' Noel said, then turned to Ryan to express his own gratitude for the afternoon's outing to the pony club. 'I'll be leaving here in a couple of days,' he went on. 'I've gathered a pile of notes on the *Montmorency*, and even obtained a copy of an old photo of her. I'll come in and say goodbye when I've booked out of the motel. You'll be home during Sunday morning?'

Ryan nodded. 'We'll be there. See you then.'

As the Range Rover moved forward Robin whimpered, 'I don't want Uncle Noel to go away.'

Judy's arm went about the boy's shoulders in a gesture of sympathy. She sensed he felt he was losing a friend.

Next morning the vivid blueness of the cloudless sky made Judy open the living-room window and draw in deep breaths of tangy sea air. A slight frost gave promise of a fine day, and as she stared towards the tall Norfolk pines their branches gave no sign of a breeze.

Ryan came to stand beside her, the fragrance of his aftershave again teasing her senses, and as usual his nearness seemed to do something to her nerves. In an effort to calm her quickening pulses she took a deep breath while forcing herself to speak casually. 'The sea looks beautiful. It's like a gigantic sheet of glass.'

Ryan smiled. 'It doesn't stay like that for long, but while it's calm I thought it might be a good idea to go for a run in the boat.'

For a moment she wondered if she'd heard him correctly, then she sent him a sharp glance. 'You mentioned a boat. What boat would this be?'

'My boat, of course. The *Dart*. She's a thirty-foot launch—a sleek craft that skims through the water with smooth speed. I keep her in the sailing club's marina. Sometimes I hitch a boat-trailer to the Range Rover's tow-bar and haul her to Lake Taupo.'

Judy felt slightly dazed. 'Really, you're full of surprises. I had no idea you owned a launch.'

'There's nothing surprising in that,' he said with a slight shrug. 'Numerous people in Napier own something that goes on the water. Or did you expect me to rush about shouting, *I've got a launch*?'

'Of course not... But...it just makes me realise I don't know you very well.'

'If you want the truth you've made it obvious you don't know me at all.' His words held a faint bitterness.

Turning to look at him, she noticed the grim line about his mouth. It was enough to tell her that, despite his friendly manner, he still resented her remarks concerning his responsibility towards Robin. 'I'm sure Robin would love to go out in a boat,' was all she could think of to say.

Ryan went on, 'I thought it might help to take his mind off ponies.' He paused, then added as an afterthought, 'And your mind too, of course.'

Her eyes widened slightly. 'My mind? What on earth are you talking about? Why would my mind be on ponies?'

'I think you know what I mean,' he returned quietly. 'Robin isn't the only one who will be sorry to see Collier leave.' He turned to regard her intently. 'Tell me—and please be honest—have you made arrangements to meet him again?' His voice had hardened.

'No, I have not,' she snapped furiously. 'Nor has there been any suggestion of it from Noel.'

'But you had ample opportunity when Robin was being given his ride,' Ryan persisted. 'What did you talk about while going round the field?'

Judy began to feel exasperated. Impatiently, she said, 'If you *must* know, he went on and on about his farm and the ponies on it. If you think any dates were made, you're very much mistaken. You could say I was playing second fiddle to a bunch of livestock, because that's where his thoughts were centred...although there were times when he spoke to Robin about the way he should be sitting.'

She turned away from him to lift the tapestry work from a nearby table, and as her needle flashed, making stitches to form white foam, she knew his eyes were still watching her. Raising her own to meet his gaze steadily, she went on, 'I know I've said things that have maddened you—'

His mouth twisted as he cut in, 'You can say *that* again! Actually, it's your line of thinking that maddens me.'

'We're not discussing that at the moment,' she argued defensively. 'It's just that I want you to know the truth as far as Noel is concerned.' She made a few more stitches, then asked, 'When do we go?'

'As soon as possible. You can put away that tapestry and we'll go before too much breeze springs up. We'll take a couple of flasks, and a bottle of drink for Robin, but we'll buy food near the marina. I'll find the picnic basket.'

Judy stuffed the tapestry back into its yellow bag, then hastened to put the kettle on. Ryan had not indicated whether or not he believed her concerning Noel, she realised, but there was little she could do about it. And she also knew what he'd meant when he'd referred to her 'line of thinking'. Of course it was his relationship to Robin. So—it maddened him, did it?

She took her own and Robin's jackets from the wardrobe, then knelt on the floor beside the boy, who was busy with his bricks. 'I've got a surprise for you,' she told him. 'We're going out in Uncle Ryan's boat, so put your bricks away.'

A short time later they were out in the bay. The sea was still calm, and the *Dart* cut through it with scarcely a ripple. The sleek craft was painted white with trimmings picked out in Prussian blue, and as she swept along the wake left behind fanned out into a wide V.

Ryan sat in a comfortable blue upholstered seat holding the wheel. Judy sat beside him in a similar seat while Robin stood between them, his small hands on the wheel. 'Look, Judy—I'm driving,' he shouted with glee. 'I'm driving a boat!'

'Aye-aye, Skipper,' she responded gaily. 'Just see that you keep clear of the rocks near the motel.' She smiled, knowing exactly whose capable hands had control of the launch, then, sending a satisfied glance towards Ryan, she added, 'I think we can guess what has just trotted over the horizon and out of somebody's mind.'

'What's the horizon?' Robin wanted to know.

'It's where the sea kisses the sky,' Ryan explained, and, to keep the boy's thoughts from anything that trotted, he added, 'I think Judy meant we should be watching that large flock of seabirds over there. They're gannets, out on a fishing expedition.'

Judy stared to where the birds were circling above what must have been a shoal of fish. 'I've never seen gannets before,' she said. 'I wish they weren't so far away.'

Ryan said, 'They're big white birds, with golden heads and black-tipped wings and tails. They dive into the sea from a height of up to a hundred feet. If we were closer you'd see them drop, with their necks extended and their long wings stretched backwards as they hit the water, and a few minutes later you'd see them shoot up with whatever they'd caught.'

Robin looked at him with wide-eyed eagerness. 'Could I find a nest, Uncle Ryan? Do they make nests in trees?'

Ryan laughed. 'No, they do not. They live on islands, where they make nests on the ground, and at Cape Kidnappers, at the southern end of this bay.' He pointed in the right direction. 'Do you see that long line of white cliffs? That's Cape Kidnappers. Suppose we let Judy steer us there…'

'*Me?*' The word escaped her like a squeak. 'I'd…I'd rock the boat.' A sudden nervousness gripped her.

'Nonsense. You'll enjoy it.' He stood up, but continued to hold the wheel. 'Get into this seat,' he commanded, with his habitual air of one who had no intention of arguing about it.

She obeyed meekly, but the bow immediately took on a will of its own, by weaving unsteadily from port to starboard, and causing Judy's nerves to collapse into a state of the jitters. 'You'd better help me,' she wailed apprehensively, while gripping the wheel. 'I...I might tip the boat over...'

'There's no need to panic,' Ryan soothed. He stood behind her seat, placed his hands over hers on the wheel, and, despite Robin's presence, rested his cheek against Judy's. The launch instantly regained its former steady course. 'Does that make you feel better?' he murmured in her ear.

'Oh, yes, it does,' she said with a sigh of relief. 'Sorry to have been such a silly twit, but I've never driven...I mean steered a launch before. The sea's not quite as calm as it was—and you did rather throw me in at the deep end.' Her tongue seemed to be running away with itself, not because of her nervousness but because of his closeness, which was putting her into a state of tension.

'You're now feeling more confident?'

She nodded, although 'confident' wasn't the word she'd have used to describe her awareness of an inner excitement caused by his touch.

'Just keep her steady on course,' he advised, and while his cheek remained against Judy's his hands left hers, to encircle her body and come to rest on her waist.

The action caused her heart to thump and her blood to race. 'Ryan—stop it,' she gasped, fearful that he might sense her arousal. 'Please—I think you'd better take over now.' She slipped into the seat she'd previously occupied.

As Ryan took control of the wheel he stared up at a gannet whirling overhead. 'Did you know that gannets mate for life?' he queried casually. 'It's more than can be said for many of the human race.'

Robin's sharp ears had caught his words. 'Mate for life—what does that mean?' he wanted to know, while looking from one to the other.

'Judy will explain,' Ryan said, while sending a teasing grin in her direction. 'I'm sure she'll find the right words.'

Judy smiled into the hazel eyes that regarded her expectantly. 'It shouldn't be too difficult,' she said. 'When two people love each other they get married...and if they keep on loving each other they stay together for as long as they live.'

Robin's gaze became steady as his little boy's voice piped a question. 'Did my mother get married?'

Startled, Judy found herself on dangerous ground. It was a question she hadn't expected—nor did she know the correct answer. Therefore she bit her lip and dodged the issue by saying, 'I've no idea, but you could ask Uncle Ryan, because he's known your mother for so much longer than I have. He's sure to know the answer.'

Ryan turned slowly to glare at Judy over the boy's head, then dodged the situation by saying in a cool tone, 'Marriage is a subject I never discuss. I'm sure Judy is well aware of that fact.'

His words held a sting that caused hurt. Don't let those moments of physical intimacy go to your head, they seemed to warn. Then, before she could indicate that she couldn't care less about Ryan's thoughts on marriage, she realised he was telling Robin a story. Fascinated, she found herself listening to it.

'It actually happened in these waters,' Ryan was saying. 'It happened more than two hundred years ago, when Captain James Cook came to New Zealand in the *Endeavour*. He was a great explorer.'

'Was his boat as big as a container ship?' Robin asked.

Ryan laughed. 'Oh, no—she was a mere three hundred and sixty-eight tons, which is very small by today's standards. Well, when Cook was anchored somewhere about here, the Maori people came in canoes to look at his ship. He hoped to talk to them, but of course he was unable to speak their language. However, he had brought with him a man from the island of Tahiti, in the Pacific, who could speak the Maori language. And, as it happened, the man from Tahiti had brought a boy from the island to act as his servant—'

'What was his name?' Robin cut in eagerly. 'Was he six—like me?'

'His name was Taiata, but he was a little older than you,' Ryan informed him gravely, while Judy turned away to hide a smile.

The story continued. 'When the Maoris saw the boy with skin the same colour as their own they became so interested they wanted to have a closer look at him. So they decided to kidnap him. Their long canoe, holding about thirty men, was drawn up beside the *Endeavour* and the Maoris who had gone on board grabbed Taiata and got him down into the canoe before Cook's men realised what was happening.

'But Taiata's yells alerted them, and as the canoe was being paddled away at great speed shots were fired across its bow from the *Endeavour*. Some of the Maoris were hit, and as they didn't have guns there was a general panic that enabled Taiata to scramble overboard and swim back to the ship. So what do you think Captain Cook named this place?'

'Cape Kidnappers,' Robin shouted in high glee. 'Uncle Ryan, you do know lots of things. Much more than Gran. I bet you know *everything*.'

Ryan's even white teeth gleamed in the sun as he threw back his head and laughed. 'Believe it or not, son, there are some things I don't know—especially concerning women.'

'Now that's an admission.' Judy tried to keep her voice flippant, but it remained unsteady due to the fact that a great truth had suddenly hit her. It had exploded into her consciousness like a blinding light, filling her with an awareness that left her feeling so bewildered she was unable to think with any degree of clarity.

It had happened while listening to the story of Taiata. Ryan's deep voice had soothed her senses, almost hypnotising her into a state of enchantment. To the boy he was like a kindly teacher, she realised, and it struck her with force that he was a man who instinctively gave to others. She'd also recognised compassion in his tone when speaking of the young Tahitian boy's frightening ordeal, and it told her he had depth of feeling for people less fortunate than himself. They were qualities that reached out to touch her...and she knew she loved him.

The knowledge left her feeling shaken, especially as she'd so recently declared herself to be finished with all men. But this was different. This was something over which she had no control, and she could only stare unseeingly at the blue sea and sky while trying to sort it out in her mind. But, however she looked at it, one thing was definite. Without a shadow of doubt she knew she wanted only one man—and that man had to be Ryan.

His voice seemed to come from a great distance. 'Where are the sandwiches? Isn't it time we ate?'

'Yes, it is.' She made an effort to pull her thoughts into some sort of order and opened the picnic basket. It was a relief to have something to do, although her hand shook slightly as she made tea.

It did not escape his notice. 'Are you OK?' he asked. 'You're looking a little pale. Not feeling seasick, I hope?'

'Not at all,' she assured him, and, although she did not feel like eating, she bit into a sandwich.

But Ryan was not satisfied. 'Then why are you looking as if the troubles of the world have suddenly descended upon your shoulders?'

It was disturbing to know her emotions were written all over her face, but quite impossible to explain why her spirits were scraping the bottom of the sea bed. Carefully, she said, 'I was just realising that next week Robin will be back at school, and...and all this will be over. It'll seem like a dream.'

There was a silence until he said, 'Are you saying you've no wish for it to be over?'

'I've enjoyed being in Napier,' she admitted guardedly. 'I love its gardens, stretching along the seafront, and the way a feature has been made of those wonderful Norfolk pines.'

'You should see them at night, when they're lit with

thousands of coloured lightbulbs,' he said. 'This evening we'll take a drive along The Parade before Robin's bedtime. It'll be a small treat for him to be out after dark.'

A treat for Robin, rather than for herself, she noticed, then told herself not to be petty. But somehow this man seemed to send her thoughts haywire, and now, watching him covertly, Judy tried to commit to memory the sight of him sitting at the wheel.

The lines of his tanned profile and clean-cut jaw came in for her scrutiny, and the way his dark auburn hair was being blown by the light breeze. And, as her eyes took in the breadth of his shoulders and muscular form of his body, she realised that here was a man of mental as well as physical vitality and strength. How on earth could she hope to forget a man like Ryan?

And then his next words amazed her. Without even glancing at her, he said casually, 'If you've really enjoyed being in Napier, why don't you spend some more time here? You could probably find a job without too much trouble—and I see no reason why you shouldn't continue to stay with me while looking for one.'

His last words made her blink, while wondering if she'd heard him correctly, and as they swept her spirits up from the sea bed she gazed at him in a searching manner. Did he really want her to stay? Or was he merely being kind? Was this the man whose burning ambition was to keep women out of his home and his heart? It was all rather puzzling, but for some unknown reason she felt it would be unwise to delve too deeply into these questions.

Ryan cut into her silence. 'Think it over,' he advised, while pouring a second cup of tea for himself.

She took a deep breath, then said impulsively, 'There's no need...I'll be very grateful to stay until I've found a job and somewhere to live. Thank you for saying I may do so.' Would Verna object to her presence? she wondered. And would there actually be a reconciliation? Surely the answer was yes—for Robin's sake.

Watching her closely, he said with perception, 'You sound happy about the idea, but your face tells me otherwise. Obviously something niggles at you.'

His tone brought a flush to her cheeks, and as it deepened she admitted hesitantly, 'I...I'm just hoping that everything will turn out well for Robin. After all, he's the one to be considered in your situation with Verna. I mean...children are so helpless when it comes to doing anything about the trauma in their lives caused by adults...' She floundered and fell silent, suddenly aware that his face had darkened with anger.

Too late, Judy recalled that the subject of Ryan's responsibility towards Robin was completely taboo—but to refuse to discuss it, she decided, was ridiculous. Nor did she like the barrier it seemed to place between them. Therefore she made an effort to pull it down by deliberately ignoring the scowl on Ryan's face.

'Robin will be fortunate to be with you,' she remarked brightly, and as though this had to be the foregone conclusion of the affair.

'Shall he indeed? What, exactly, do you mean by that?' His face had become a mask, the olive-green eyes hooded.

'Well...' She struggled to find something to say. 'You're full of general knowledge. You'll be a wonderful help when he's doing his school homework...' Something in his expression caused her words to dwindle, and she could now see that she'd really annoyed him.

The look on his face had become thunderous. His mouth had tightened into a hard line of thin lips which scarcely moved as he rasped furiously, 'I can see you've got your mind well and truly made up about a certain situation. Nor do you have a hell of a lot of faith in people. You can come close...yet continue to think the worst.'

She was dismayed by his outburst, and, taken aback, she quavered, 'Wh-what do you mean?'

'If you can't see what I mean you'd better forget it,' he snarled.

'No, I'll not forget it,' she protested indignantly. 'What I've said has been harmless enough. I can't see why it should've infuriated you to such an extent.'

'It's what you think—what you're so damned sure about—that makes me mad,' he gritted, while glaring at her. 'Hell's bells! Surely you can work it out for yourself?'

'No, I'm afraid I can't,' she flashed at him, while frustration caused her temper to rise.

But he made no attempt to enlighten her. He merely swung the launch round in a wide circle, then made the motor roar while heading back towards the channel leading into the marina. His face as he stared ahead was grim, and even Robin sensed that all was not well.

'Why are you so angry with Judy, Uncle Ryan?' the boy's high treble queried above the sound of the motor. 'I don't like you being angry with Judy.'

Relaxing slightly, Ryan sent the boy a kindly glance as he said, 'I'm afraid you wouldn't understand, son. It's just one of those things that happen between grown-ups.'

Robin said, 'I think you've made Judy sad. Why don't you kiss her better like you always do?'

Ryan turned away from him. 'Can't you see I'm busy at the wheel? Remember those rocks at the channel entrance? I have to watch very carefully when getting past them.' He paused thoughtfully, then added in a serious tone, 'Of course, you could kiss Judy for me.'

'A boy on a man's errand,' Judy was goaded to put in, the remark slipping out before she could control her tongue. Until this moment she'd been sitting huddled in misery, the sound of the motor throbbing in her ears like a drum. Everything had been so pleasant until she'd opened her stupid mouth once too often. For heaven's sake—what had she said to have annoyed Ryan to this extent? Scraps of their recent conversation flitted through her mind, but she could see no connection between homework and trust.

And then Robin's little arms reached to embrace her, his

face raised as he said, 'Don't be sad, Judy. I'll kiss you better...I'll kiss you just like Uncle Ryan does.'

'Thank you, darling.' Judy hugged him closely, then met Ryan's eyes above the boy's head. It was too much for either of them. Judy giggled and Ryan chuckled, then their tension fell away as they both began to laugh. It was enough to lighten the atmosphere and to sweep Ryan's anger away before it ruined the day's outing.

A short time later they arrived home to discover Kate Coster about to put the vacuum cleaner away. She had also returned Ryan's laundry and had placed an apple pie in the fridge.

'Thank you, Kate,' Ryan said appreciatively.

'I'm not neglecting you just because you've got a woman in the house,' Kate said with an air of virtue. 'And by the way, there was a phone call from the lady at Te Pohue. She said to tell you that Neddy, the donkey, has a new home. He'll be taken away tomorrow.'

'I see.' Ryan's face had become expressionless and he spoke in a bland tone. 'Was there anything else?'

'She told me to remind you that the new school term begins next week.' Kate flicked a glance towards Robin, who watched her apprehensively from behind Judy. Then, avoiding the latter's eye, Kate went on, 'She also asked me to let her know when your house is free of guests. Do you want me to do that?' she demanded uncompromisingly.

'I think I'm capable of imparting such information myself,' Ryan returned smoothly. 'Thank you for taking the messages.'

'Right. I'll be off, then...'

Kate's departure left a tense silence in the room, and as Judy left it to attend to the mugs and plates in the picnic basket she became filled with anxiety. Why hadn't Ryan told Kate the house wouldn't be free of a guest until she herself had found a job and somewhere else to live? Did this mean the tiff out in the launch had caused him to change his mind about the invitation?

A feeling of disappointment invaded her, and in an effort to disguise it she went to the dining alcove table and bent her head over the tapestry work. Should she ask him for a direct answer? she wondered. At least she'd know where she stood.

'Something is niggling at you?' Ryan queried softly.

Startled, she looked up to discover him watching her. 'Why would you say that?'

'Because your face says it all.'

'My face says *what*?' she demanded with defiance.

'That I'll go back on my word. That I'll let you know— in the nicest possible way, of course—that I've changed my mind about your staying here.' Ryan's tone had become clipped.

'How can you possibly know what I'm thinking?' she hedged, feeling dismay because his assumption of her thoughts had been right on target.

He gave a short laugh. 'It's not too difficult. I have only to recall your constant doubting of my integrity and your more than obvious belief in my lack of responsibility towards a certain small party.' The words were flung at her accusingly.

'Then you admit it?'

'I admit nothing. But it maddens me when other people condemn me without knowing the facts...' He stared at her searchingly. 'Incidentally, what made you so sure I'd go back on my word? I notice you haven't denied it.'

'I just thought that...that with somebody else in the house...you...you wouldn't want me to be here...'

'Suppose you worry about that problem when you actually *see* somebody else in the house,' he suggested sardonically.

She nodded. 'OK, I'll do that.' Then, having no wish to discuss a matter which might betray her feelings for him, Judy glanced at her watch and said, 'If we're going out to see the lights, I'd better do something about an early evening meal. Robin mustn't be too late out of bed.'

'You're quite right, little mother.'

Judy left him and went to the kitchen, his last words almost overwhelming her with a feeling of frustration. Little mother, indeed. Was that the only way he could see her? Well, her period of being a 'little mother' to another woman's child was almost over, but—with a little bit of luck—she'd find a job in Napier and get her life back to normal living.

That was if she could ever discover a state of normal living. Loving Ryan as she did seemed to have placed her in a position where the peace of normality seemed to lie in a remote area and well out of sight. Was she destined to live with the ache of always mentally reaching for him, but never finding him there?

It was almost seven o'clock by the time Ryan opened the doors of the Range Rover for Judy and Robin. The winter evening was now quite dark as they drove along the seafront towards the Port, which was ablaze with lights from ships and buildings. Lights also gleamed from houses on the hillsides, but these paled into insignificance when they reached the display of coloured bulbs laced through the branches of the tall Norfolk pines edging the city waterfront.

Ryan parked the vehicle beneath the spreading boughs of one of them, then led Judy and Robin into the gardens stretching between The Parade and the sea. A waning moon did its best to brighten a star-studded sky, and despite being winter the cold was not intense. He reached to take her hand while guiding her along a path, then sent her a questioning glance as her fingers tightened upon his own. 'Are you all right?' he queried. 'Not feeling nervous through being out in the dark in unfamiliar territory?'

'Not while I'm with you.' Her fingers gripped his even more tightly, almost as though seeking security through his vitality and strength. Then, in an effort to excuse her action, she gave a shaky laugh while gazing up at the colourful magic in the trees. 'The lights seem to have gone to my head,' she said. 'It's all so lovely. I do hope I find a job in Napier.'

He stared at her through the gloom, the expression on his face becoming serious. 'The lights make you feel that way? Believe it or not, I imagined it had something to do with my humble self.'

She was quick to respond. 'Oh, yes, it has…you've become a very good friend. But the time will come when you'll forget I was even around. Your life will be back to normal.'

'Is that a fact?'

But before he could say more Judy realised that Robin was no longer beside her. 'Where is he? *Where is he?*' she gasped, while turning left and right to peer through the gloom.

'Don't panic,' Ryan soothed. 'There are swings a short distance along this path. He discovered them while you were considering the trees—'

'But he shouldn't be alone,' Judy cut in. 'There could be strange men…' The warning issued by Hilda Simmons flooded back into her mind, causing her to run along the path towards the distant screech of a squeaking swing.

But there was little need for concern. When they discovered Robin he was enjoying himself. He'd found a friend, who had joined him on a roundabout and whose father had supplied each boy with a small bar of chocolate. Robin's was already half eaten, and when he saw Judy the remainder was stuffed into his mouth.

Standing on the edge of the small play area, Ryan laid a detaining hand on Judy's arm. 'Let him have a short time with another kid,' he advised. 'He's had nobody to play with since he's been here. As for the chocolate, it won't put his teeth into a basin just yet.'

'I'm more worried about him being sick in the night,' Judy said ruefully, then became aware that Ryan had drawn her into the deeper shadows of an evergreen tree. In this place of concealment his arms held her against him. The feel of his breath on her forehead told her his head was lowered, and because she had no power to resist him she raised her face to meet his lips.

It was a gentle kiss that told her he had himself under control. Even so, his mouth played seductively with her lips, then, like a butterfly flitting from one petal to another, touched her cheeks, her lids and her brow. Her heart thumped, and as her pulses raced she longed for him to display a little of the passion she knew he was holding on a tight rein.

As though reading her thoughts, he murmured huskily, 'Now is neither the time nor the place. And I'll tell you something else, Judy Arledge, I'll be damned glad when the responsibility of that boy has been removed from your shoulders.'

Pulling herself together, she was struck by the thought of his own six-year lack of responsibility, then found herself raking her mind to find excuses for him. Loving him, she felt sure there must be a reason somewhere—*if only he'd tell her about it*. As for asking him—no way would she raise the question.

She was feeling depressed, and a deep sigh escaped her as she said, 'I can't understand why Robin's mother hasn't arrived before this time.'

Ryan shrugged. 'Some people can be very unreliable. However, the boy must go back to school. It means that on Monday you must catch a flight and return him to Christchurch.'

'Yes, I suppose so,' Judy admitted in a dull tone. Mentally, she felt as if she'd been dismissed from Ryan's mind. A few minutes ago he'd kissed her, but now it sounded as if he couldn't care less whether she stayed or not. In fact she was filled with a horrible suspicion that he'd prefer her to leave. A ball of ice began to form within her breast, its chill making her feel thoroughly miserable.

Had he forgotten that he'd suggested she should find a job in Napier and that she could stay with him while doing so? Why hadn't he said, *But you'll be coming back?* Why had those words remained unspoken? You're being a fool, she told herself. You're expecting too much from him— much more than he's willing to give.

And then a commotion from the play area caught their attention. Robin's new friend appeared to be having an argument with his father. Dad, it seemed, was ready to go home—whereas the boy was not.

Ryan solved the problem. He drew Judy from the shadows of the tree that had been concealing them, and spoke to Robin in a voice of stern authority. 'Come along, lad, it's time to go home to bed.'

Robin could see that his new friend was about to be dragged away from this place of swings and roundabouts. He came at once, and on the way home told them about Joe. Did Uncle Ryan think he'd be able to see Joe again? Joe was six—just like him.

Judy noticed that Ryan avoided a negative reply by just being noncommittal. It also made her realise that the time for departure to Christchurch would come soon, and that Robin had clothes to be washed.

On arrival home she became busy with the task, feeling grateful that it gave her something to do. At least it prevented her from looking as though she hoped for more kisses from Ryan.

Later, as she lay wide-eyed in the darkness of her bedroom, she recalled the casual way in which Ryan had said she must take Robin home. Of course he was right—the boy had to begin the new school term. But as there'd been no mention of her return to Napier, she wondered if she'd be wise to do so.

Reviewing the situation, she tried to be honest with herself, and, despite any signs to the contrary, one fact shouted aloud. Ryan did not want a woman in his house. He'd made that clear from the moment of her arrival. He'd turned it into a hermit's cave, and that was how he wanted it to remain. His invitation to her had been nothing more than a spur-of-the-moment kindness. Or, worse, a way of taking their relationship to the next level. Ryan was a man after all—with a man's needs. It was clear that he wasn't satisfied with just kisses. All he was offering was a temporary affair—the only guarantee she would have would be a broken heart when it all came to an end. If Judy had any sense at all she'd remain in Christchurch and forget Ryan—if she could. Unable to stop herself, she wept, and her tears began to soak into her pillow.

CHAPTER EIGHT

WHEN Judy woke next morning she still felt dull and depressed. Rain had fallen during the early hours, and now the grey sky and the grey sea reflected her mood. She knew she should spring out of bed, but before emerging from its warmth she lay contemplating the packing to be done. It would include coping with the books Ryan had bought for Robin, and all those bricks. There seemed to be hundreds of them.

Eventually she dragged herself from the bed and looked in the mirror. 'You look a mess,' she muttered, frowning at the shadows beneath her eyes. 'You'd better do something about that face, and right smartly. People in love are supposed to be elated and look happy.' But only if that love is returned, she conceded as an afterthought.

However, an improvement was achieved by using extra make-up and by putting on a warm skirt and top in pale gold. Privately, she always looked upon it as her sunshine outfit. She knew the colour suited her, and in some strange way it always seemed to give her spirits a push upward.

When she entered the kitchen Robin's eyes became round with surprise. Despite a mouthful of toast, he demanded, 'Why are you wearing your best dress, Judy?'

She laughed dismissively. 'Who says it's my best dress?'

Ryan, who had stood up at her entrance, swept an admiring glance over her. 'Best or otherwise—you're looking very charming.' His eyes narrowed slightly as he observed her more closely, then he drawled with a hint of mockery, 'Would there be a reason for you being all dressed up? Could it be because a certain gentleman is expected to arrive this morning?'

'Certainly not,' she flashed at him in a cool tone, then, because she felt tired and somewhat worn out, she added thoughtlessly, 'I always like to dress up when I'm feeling down...' The words dwindled as she became annoyed with herself for having made that admission.

Ryan took her up on it. 'Why are you feeling down? Is it because that same certain gentleman is about to depart?'

Judy stared at him blankly, while trying to control her irritation.

Robin piped up with an explanation. 'Uncle Ryan means Uncle Noel. Uncle Ryan says you'll be baking this morning—special for Uncle Noel.'

'Then he's mistaken,' Judy retorted, with more heat than she had intended to betray. 'I shall not be baking, especially for Uncle Noel. Digestive biscuits will be quite suitable with his coffee. In any case, I'd forgotten he was coming.' The last words were spoken loftily.

Ryan swept another glance over her. 'You'd forgotten he was coming to say goodbye? You could've fooled me.' His tone echoed disbelief, and there was also a sardonic twist to his sensuous lips.

Noticing it, Judy said, 'Are you accusing me of lying to you? Or are you just mad with me for some reason? Not that there's anything unusual about *that*.'

His eyes became hooded. 'What do you mean?'

'Well—you seem to be harbouring a grudge where I'm concerned. It's like a continual undercurrent of annoyance, and if you think I'm unaware of it you're mistaken.'

'You're saying I'm never nice to you?' he drawled.

A flush sent a rosy hue into her cheeks. 'That's what puzzles me. When you forget yourself you're *very* nice,' she admitted frankly. 'But then something happens and you shut me out.' She closed her mouth abruptly. *Watch it, or he'll guess how you feel about him,* she warned herself.

Ryan observed her through narrowed lids. 'Go on— something tells me you have more on your mind,' he urged softly.

'Only the many things that must be done today.'

'Things like what?' Ryan queried.

'Like packing to return to Christchurch tomorrow. You yourself suggested it last night, if you care to remember.' The reminder came sweetly, while she watched Ryan stare at her in glum silence, and, although she longed to hear him say, *But you'll be back soon*, again the words did not come. After a pause she said, 'I'll make a start on Robin's suitcase after breakfast.'

Her last words brought a sudden wail from Robin. His eyes filled and his lip quivered as he began to weep, while saying brokenly, 'I don't want to go home to Christchurch. I want to stay here with Uncle Ryan—I like being here with Uncle Ryan.'

Judy was not surprised by the outburst. She put her arms about Robin and tried to explain gently. 'Darling, you must listen to me. You and I have caused enough disruption for Uncle Ryan. He's been very patient about it all, but now it's time for us to let him get on with his own life and all the things he needs to do.'

But Robin wasn't listening. He pushed Judy's arms away, then went to stand beside Ryan's chair. The tears fell even faster as he began to plead between sobs, 'Please, Uncle Ryan...*please, Uncle Ryan*...can I stay with you? I don't want to stay with Gran. She's crabby...she's most awful crabby...'

Ryan frowned, his expression becoming concerned. 'But your mother is there,' he pointed out patiently.

'Not at the moment... *Please*, Uncle Ryan...I want to live here with you.' Robin's face was pathetic.

Judy's heart went out to the boy. She was well aware of the hard time he had with his grandmother, even if Hilda Simmons meant well. The sight of him pleading with this man, who, she felt sure, was his father, was something she had not expected to witness, and she felt deeply saddened. Tears threatened to fall, causing her to blink rapidly.

It also upset her to see Ryan placed in this situation.

Studying his face, she could see only compassion for the boy, but otherwise he remained strongly in command of his emotions. He's got a powerful grip on himself, she thought with reluctant admiration. If only he would acknowledge his relationship to the lad, but obviously he had no intention of doing so, and again her love for him told her he must have a reason.

The scene was becoming almost more than Judy could bear, when Ryan asked Robin a question that changed matters. His face bland, he leaned back in his chair and stared at the ceiling. 'I suppose you remember Miss Coster, my housekeeper?' he queried. 'You haven't seen much of her because she usually comes when we're out.'

Robin nodded while taking tissues from Judy. 'She's crabby too,' he sniffed. 'I gave her a hard kick.'

'Got her fair and square on the shin, if I remember correctly. Of course she'll be here every day,' Ryan informed him casually.

Robin's mouth sagged open as he stared at Ryan in wide-eyed horror. Aghast, he quavered plaintively, 'I don't want to be here with *her*. I don't like her. Why does she have to be here?'

'Because she cleans the house and washes my clothes.' Ryan grinned.

'Can't Judy do all those things?' Robin demanded.

'Certainly not. Judy hopes to find a job. She'll be busy working in one place or another,' Ryan informed him.

One place or another, Judy thought dolefully—but which place would it be? Christchurch or Napier? And was Ryan being deliberately vague? After all it had been he who'd suggested she should find a job in Napier.

Robin heaved a sigh of dejection. 'I suppose I gotta go home to Gran and Mum,' he muttered morosely.

Ryan's voice held sympathy. 'Well, it's like this, son— better the devil you know than the devil you don't. When you're a grown-up you'll realise you can't have everything you want.'

Judy gave a soft laugh as she spoke to him gently. 'I must say you haven't done too badly of late. Not many boys in your class at school will have been out in a boat or had pony rides this holiday. And just look at all those books and bricks you'll be taking home. He's really been a most wonderful...uncle.' Her gaze rested on Ryan steadily as she uttered the last words.

Ryan's mouth tightened as he glared at her. 'You never give up, do you?' he gritted icily.

'It's just that I feel deeply about the situation...'

He cut in angrily. 'What you hope to achieve by these snide remarks is beyond my comprehension. I'm going to my office.' He stood up abruptly and left the room.

Judy knew it was Ryan's use of the word 'son' that had got to her. Even so, she cursed herself for being a fool. Why on earth do you keep rubbing it in? she asked herself peevishly. You'll never get anywhere by doing so. But in her heart she longed to see Ryan do the right thing by Robin. This man, who was so perfect in every other respect, seemed to have this one flaw, and, loving him, she wanted to see it wiped away.

Despondently, she cleared the breakfast dishes, then found Robin's suitcase and laid it open on the bed. As she packed everything she could into it her thoughts returned to the boy's tearful plea to live with Ryan. Robin, she realised, had forgotten his earlier controversy with Kate Coster. To have reminded him of it had been nothing less than a stroke of genius on Ryan's part, Judy decided, while moving into the next room to make a start on her own suitcase.

She was bending over it when Ryan spoke to her from the doorway. 'There's no need for panic,' he pointed out. 'Your plane doesn't leave before tomorrow afternoon. Come and relax in the living room.'

The suggestion heartened her as it meant he'd got over the most recent vexation she had caused. However, instead of complying at once, she said, 'I'm wondering how to get

Robin's books and toys home. There are too many for the suitcases.'

'That's no problem,' Ryan said. He disappeared, then returned with a well-worn holdall, which he handed to her. 'There's no need to return this. I've no wish to see it again.' His tone was abrupt.

'Thank you.' She wondered a little about his terseness. It was almost as though the bag evoked bitter memories and he'd be glad to see it leave the house—just as he'd be glad to see *her* leave the house. And though she gave no indication of the latter thought it filled her with a deep depression.

When she reached the living room she went to where she'd left the tapestry on the alcove dining table. The work was spilling out of its yellow plastic bag, and, grateful for something to do, she threaded the needle with sea-green wool. Should she take it with her? Or would it prove to be something better left behind? At one time she'd thought it would be a happy souvenir of this place, but now it could only be a painful reminder. The knowledge settled the question. She'd leave it behind with the suggestion that Ryan should give it to Kate.

The decision had just been reached when the front door-bell echoed through the house. Robin, searching beneath the settee for hidden bricks, sprang to his feet. 'That'll be Uncle Noel,' he said to Ryan. 'May I go down and open the door for him?'

'Of course. Ask him to come upstairs.' Then he spoke rapidly to Judy. 'I presume you've already made arrangements for you and Noel to meet again?'

She gaped at him, then said furiously, 'Have you forgotten that he's going north, and that tomorrow I'll be going south?'

'That's no problem with daily flights.'

'If it weren't so ridiculous I'd almost imagine you were jealous,' she snapped, then fell silent as voices floated up from the front hall.

Noel, it seemed, was not alone. He was accompanied by a woman whose voice, Judy thought, was surprisingly like Verna's. The sound of it gave her a shock, causing her to stand up slowly and stare at the living-room door while waiting for them to appear on the landing.

Robin rushed up the stairs ahead of them. Breathless with excitement, he exclaimed, 'My mummy's here, Uncle Ryan...my mummy's here...'

Ryan had also heard the female voice. Suddenly alert, he had risen from the chair in which he'd been reclining, and as the woman walked into the room he drawled with cool nonchalance, 'So, you've arrived at last, Verna.'

Verna was a tall, dark-haired woman, vaguely similar to her mother, but without the domineering attitude that hit most people when they met Hilda Simmons. She was handsome rather than beautiful, and it was easy to see from whom Robin had inherited his hazel eyes. She sent Judy a casual nod, then spoke to Ryan with a disarming smile. 'I believe you've already met Frank.'

'Frank?' Ryan's dark brows drew together, his jaw tightening as he looked questioningly at Noel. 'I don't understand. What is this?'

Noel had the grace to look apologetic, and even embarrassed. 'I'm normally known as Frank Bryant,' he admitted. 'I would've told you if I hadn't been in a damned awkward situation. I wanted to see the boy, but I was afraid that if you learnt my true identity you might follow his grandmother's caper of smuggling him away to some other place.'

Ryan eyed him narrowly. 'Are you saying your name isn't Collier?'

'My name is Francis Noel Collier Bryant, which is a bit of a mouthful. I simply used my two middle names. Collier was my mother's name.' He regarded Ryan steadily as he asked, 'Do you think you can forgive the deception? I'm sure you'll understand why I felt it to be so necessary.'

'I dare say I'll get over it,' Ryan conceded dryly. He turned to Verna. 'When did you arrive from Christchurch?'

'Yesterday. Frank met me at the airport. Last night I stayed at the motel. I've known him for years. Naturally he's...he's very interested in Robin.' Verna's words were accompanied by a significant look as a slight flush rose to her cheeks.

'So it would seem, nor, now, is it difficult to guess why.' Ryan's tone had become sardonic. 'Please sit down and tell me more. I believe I'm beginning to see the light, although I must say I've been damned slow about it.'

Judy was also beginning to see the light, and the shock was keeping her silent. *Ryan was not Robin's father*, and the fact hit her with force. She'd felt so sure about it, yet she'd been so wrong. Noel—Frank, she amended mentally—was Robin's father. Verna had come to meet *him* in Napier—not to be reconciled with Ryan. It all became clear in her dazed mind as she listened to Frank's explanation.

'My cousin's child, Sally, told Robin her uncle Frank had come to visit them,' he said. 'Robin told his grandmother. She knew exactly who Uncle Frank was, and with Verna away skiing she began to panic. She was afraid I'd grab him and take him to Cambridge, so she made arrangements for him to be whipped off to Napier. Apparently, you were the only one she could turn to.'

Ryan said, 'I gathered there was a crisis, but I could make neither head nor tail of it.'

Frank went on, 'Fortunately Robin told Sally he was going to stay at Napier with Uncle Ryan. And luckily I was able to get on the same flight. As for the *Montmorency*, I've been meaning to research her details for some time, so it fitted in nicely.'

Judy spoke for the first time since the visitors' arrival. 'Would you have swept him off to Cambridge?' she asked, her curiosity getting the better of her. No wonder this man had helped her with Robin on the plane. But how was she to have guessed him to be the stranger Hilda had feared?

Frank said, 'I wouldn't have taken him without his mother's consent, but I was longing to talk to him and get to know him. I had gone to Christchurch with the sole purpose of talking to Verna about our getting together again. I've already told you about my earlier circumstances. Years ago, when I first met her, my prospects were poor. Her mother ordered me out of the house. She called me an unemployed stableboy.'

Verna spoke ruefully. 'At that time Frank's situation at his home wasn't the best. I doubt that I'd have been welcome at Cambridge. But now everything has changed, and today he's taking Robin and me back to his farm.'

Ryan's lips twitched as he asked a question. 'Your mother—how is she taking this change of affairs?'

'Very badly, I'm afraid. Mother is not amused—but I'd rather not talk about the row we had,' Verna admitted.

Robin, who had been staring at Frank wide-eyed, now moved to stand beside his chair. He looked bewildered as he asked timidly, 'Do I have to call you Uncle Frank now...'stead of Uncle Noel?'

Frank dragged him on to his knee. 'Do you think you could try calling me Dad instead?' he asked a little gruffly.

'Are you really my *father*?' Robin's hushed tones echoed wonderment.

'Yes, son—I am.' Frank's arms went about the boy and Robin clung to him. There was silence in the room while they hugged each other, until Frank found it necessary to wipe his eyes and blow his nose.

It was too much for Judy. A lump formed in her throat, almost choking her, and she knew that if she didn't pull herself together she'd begin to weep from the sheer happiness of knowing that Robin had found his real father. 'I'll make coffee,' she said shakily, then hurried to the kitchen where she dabbed at her eyes.

Verna followed her. 'Anything I can do to help?' she asked.

Judy placed biscuits on a plate while waiting for the water to boil. 'Not really—although I'd like to know what took you so long to get here. We've been expecting you for days.'

'Preparing to leave Christchurch for good took time,' Verna explained.

'Yes, I suppose it would. Then...you're not married?' Judy put the question hesitantly.

'No. But after last night at the motel we probably shall be married quite soon.' The smile that spread over Verna's face made her look almost beautiful.

'I'm sure everything will turn out well,' Judy assured her warmly. She felt happy for Verna, and happy for Robin and Frank. Now they were a family, which was as it should be.

Verna continued, in a voice that was full of gratitude, 'I don't know how to begin thanking you for taking care of Robin. He looks so well.'

Judy spoke emphatically. 'It's Ryan you have to thank. He's been wonderful to him. He's treated him like a son— in fact to such an extent I felt sure that Robin *was* his son.' She bit her lip, feeling guilty about this.

'Well, he isn't,' Verna assured her vehemently. 'Why do you think I used the name Bryant? I knew exactly whose child he was.' She paused, then added diffidently, 'When we've had our coffee would you mind putting his things together? You'll know where they are and what he's got.'

Judy gave a small laugh. 'They're already packed. I intended taking him home tomorrow.' She drew a quick breath, while realising that the entire situation had now changed. There was no longer any need for her to go to Christchurch, and this was something she'd have to think about. But not at the moment. Later, when her mind was clear. And, pushing the question aside, she carried the tray of steaming coffee mugs to the alcove table.

Verna followed with the plate of biscuits, and as she reached the table she noticed the tapestry. It brought an exclamation from her. 'Good grief—it's the cushion cover I was making. Have you been working on it?'

'I needed something to do,' Judy explained. 'You'd better take it with you. You could have it framed as a picture.'

'Yes, I'll do that. I bought it after Frank told me his people had come to New Zealand on the *Montmorency*.' Verna's face had become a deep pink.

Judy pushed the work and its wools into the yellow bag, then carried it to Robin's room, where she stuffed it into the holdall. Was Verna recalling the day she'd thrown the lot at Ryan? she wondered.

After that there didn't seem to be a great deal to say, and as the visitors had a lengthy drive ahead of them they decided to leave soon after finishing their coffee. Robin's luggage was carried downstairs, and it was then that they saw that Frank's rental car had a double horse-trailer attached to its tow-bar.

'You made purchases?' Ryan asked.

Frank grinned. 'I've bought Bluebell, and I've also bought Neddy, to accompany her on the way home. They travel better in pairs. I'm collecting them both from the paddock at Cynthia's cottage on our way through Te Pohue.'

Robin's eyes became round as he almost choked with excitement. 'Cor, Dad—are we taking Bluebell with us?'

'That's right, son. She's your new pony. Now thank Uncle Ryan and Judy for all they've done for you, then get into the car.'

Robin obeyed immediately. He skipped about from sheer elation, forgetting any sadness he might have at leaving Judy and his uncle Ryan in his delight at discovering he had not just a new daddy but a pony too! In some strange way Judy felt that his days of tantrums might be over.

Moments later the car drove away, the empty horse-trailer swaying slightly as it was drawn along. And as the vehicle disappeared towards the highway that would take them over the hills Judy dared to look at Ryan. She found his face to be inscrutable, and she couldn't help wondering about his thoughts. Tentatively, she said, 'Noel...I mean Frank...was a surprise.'

'Not so surprising now that I'm giving it a little more thought. Didn't I tell you I felt there was something about him...something I couldn't put my finger on?' He turned on his heel and went indoors.

Judy followed him up the stairs. 'Has it upset you?' she asked a little breathlessly as she reached the top.

He swung round to face her. 'Has what upset me?'

'That...that Verna left so soon. I mean...you haven't seen her for years, and you hardly had time for more than a few words.'

'Which were all I needed, thank you very much. In any case, it was Frank who had some explaining to do. However, I hope they'll be happy.'

Judy spoke warmly. 'I'm glad you feel like that. Were you actually engaged to Verna all those years ago?' This was something she felt she had to know, and the question was put guilelessly, as she hoped she wouldn't be told to mind her own business.

For a brief moment Ryan looked at her in a manner which suggested he had a good mind to do just that, but instead he gave a small shrug as he said, 'No, I hadn't put a ring on her finger, if that's what you mean, but I was thinking about it. I'd reached the stage of believing that Verna and I would get along pretty well, but possibly that was because I was becoming tired of living alone.' He uttered a small oath, as though becoming impatient with himself, then strode into the kitchen and refilled their coffee mugs.

Placing Judy's mug on the dining table, he stood staring moodily through the alcove window, his dark brows drawn together. Looking back into the past, he went on in a low voice, 'It happened when I was visiting Christchurch fairly frequently. They were business trips, concerned with the buying of packing materials for sending fruit overseas. Needless to say I saw a fair amount of Verna...'

'Of course,' Judy murmured during a silence, while Ryan sipped his coffee. She could imagine them going to parties and out to dinner.

'I don't know why I'm telling you this,' he complained in a grumbling tone. 'I've never told anybody else.'

'It's good to talk,' she reminded him gently, while fearing he might change his mind about doing so. 'Was that when you became...close?'

'I suppose you could say so,' he admitted reluctantly. 'On the last occasion I had to visit Verna just after breakfast, because I had a plane to catch. She seemed to be preoccupied with needlework.'

'You mean—the tapestry?'

'Right. I was surprised because she'd told me she hated all types of sewing, and even this appeared to be an effort.' Ryan's face cleared as he gave a sudden burst of laughter, then he continued to chuckle as he went on, 'And then the dragon came into the room. She told me that poor Verna wasn't at all well. Every morning she was ill.'

Enlightenment dawned upon Judy, her tone becoming hushed as she said, 'Don't tell me, let me guess... *morning sickness*?'

Ryan nodded. 'The mere mention of it was enough to send Verna rushing to the bathroom. While she was there the dragon told me she was very happy for us both. Also that she hoped we'd be married as soon as possible, and before Verna became too large to wear a suitable wedding dress. She herself had already put a deposit on a pram. Would I please be good enough to reimburse her for it, and pay the remainder of the money owing?' He began to chuckle again.

Judy felt shocked. 'I'll bet it was no laughing matter at the time.'

'It was not. I told the dragon she had to be out of her mind. I assured her that in no way could Verna's pregnancy be laid at my door. Then, when Verna returned to the room, the enormity of the situation hit me with real force. I'd been about to ask her to marry me and she was carrying another man's child. I pressed her for details of his identity, but she told me nothing. We had a colossal row, which ended when she threw the tapestry at me. I picked it up and stuffed it into my holdall.'

Judy sent him a sharp glance. 'The same holdall now carrying Robin's bricks and books?'

He nodded. 'The same. I was more than pleased to see it go.'

She gave a small laugh. 'Well, it's also carrying the tapestry on its way to Cambridge.'

'Best place for it.' Ryan made his way to a chair, where he relaxed with the air of one who had unburdened himself.

Judy hesitated to ask the question simmering in the back of her mind, but it was something else she had to know. 'Have you any feelings left for Verna?' she queried in a low voice.

'None at all, although they took a long time to die. I pushed her out of my mind by concentrating on work. I took no interest in women because I considered the entire sex to be untrustworthy. Believe me, I became a bitter individual. Kate was right when she dubbed this house the hermit's cave.'

Judy looked at him with understanding. 'I'm glad you've told me about what happened. It's been like a half-finished jigsaw, but now you've completed the picture for me. As for bitterness, I doubt that you have an atom of it left.'

'What makes you so sure about that?' His lids had become hooded.

'Well, you took Robin in, didn't you? As far as you were concerned he was no ordinary child. He was *that particular child*.'

'Thank you for having at least that much faith in my character...I mean about my not being full of bitterness. However, you might as well know there are other things that infuriate me.'

'Things—like what?'

'Like having my integrity questioned. That really makes me *mad*.' His last words sounded like a low snarl. 'I was hoping you'd give me the benefit of the doubt, but I see not the slightest sign of it,' he gritted icily.

His tone made Judy straighten her back. 'The...the doubt? What on earth are you talking about?' she demanded indignantly. There was something here she didn't like, and although she was unable to sort it out in her mind, one point seemed to be clear. His anger was aimed directly at her. 'I'm afraid I don't understand. Would you please be more explicit?' she asked with forced sweetness.

'OK, I'll spell it out,' he rasped. 'For almost the entire period of your visit here you've looked upon me as being a man who would desert a woman and the child he'd fathered.'

Mentally, Judy was knocked sideways by the accusation. A gasp escaped her as colour left her face, then guilt sent it flooding back into her cheeks. But before she could say anything Ryan's next words made her ears ring. They were loaded with reproach.

'You assumed—and decided—that for the last six years I've dodged my responsibilities towards young Robin while allowing Verna to exist as a single mother. Don't bother to deny it because at times it's been written all over your face. In fact there have been times when you've almost blurted it out at me. And let me tell you I've damned well resented it,' he added fiercely.

Judy felt horrified that she had been so obvious, and now she almost cringed beneath the wrath that had been released. She could find nothing to say, mainly because his accusations were true. She *had* decided he was Robin's father, but she'd also had plenty of reason to reach that conclusion. In defence, she said with a hint of defiance, 'OK, if you want the truth, I *did* think you were Robin's father but it was *you* who planted the idea in my head.'

'What rubbish is this?' he scoffed. 'I never said anything that could possibly cause you to believe—'

She cut in, 'It was not only what you said—it was also what you did. You were so thoughtful and generous towards him. You acted just like a loving father. Did you ever count the times you called him *son*? What else was I to think?'

He was startled. 'I did? I called him son?'

'Sometimes you called him lad,' she conceded, while trying to be accurate, 'but there were numerous times when you called him son. It's a wonder he didn't ask questions about it.'

'I assure you, it was only a figure of speech,' he declared firmly.

Her brows rose. 'Really? Well, I'm afraid my psychic powers aren't strong enough for me to have been positive about that fact. Besides, haven't you told me you're a man who means what he says? Naturally, I thought you meant son *literally*.' She was beginning to feel a sense of relief—as though she was finally dispelling his previous anger—until his next words dragged her down again.

Morosely, he said, 'I think it was your remark out on the boat that really got to me. I'd be a wonderful help with Robin's homework, you said. It confirmed all my suspicions about your thoughts.'

'My concern was for Robin,' she admitted, while beginning to feel miserable. 'He's only a little boy; he needs both his parents.'

His tone became sardonic. 'Was your concern also for Verna? Were you trying to get her installed in this house? Please be honest.'

'I...I did wonder about a reconciliation...'

'That'd be the day,' he cut in with a ferocious snarl.

Suddenly Judy's patience deserted her. 'OK, OK—so I was wrong,' she exclaimed vehemently. 'If you were smart enough to read my thoughts, why didn't you tell me I was wrong? Why didn't you tell me you knew I imagined you to be Robin's father, but that I was making a mighty big mistake?'

'Because I didn't want to *have* to tell you. I wanted you to have *faith* in me. I wanted you to *trust* me, but it seemed impossible for you to do either,' he gritted on a harsh note.

Judy's blue eyes became shadowed pools of anguish. She knew she loved him, yet she'd failed him. She also knew she'd hurt him deeply, and, while she longed to fling her arms about him in an effort to make amends, she feared her gesture of comfort would betray her true feelings towards him. After all, she had to retain *some* pride.

It was no wonder he hadn't reminded her she'd be coming back to Napier, she decided. Obviously he'd changed his mind about that because he no longer wanted her to come back. 'I can only say I'm sorry,' she mumbled, then gave an uncontrolled sigh, adding, 'I'd better finish packing my suitcase.'

'OK, you do that,' he returned calmly. 'As for me—I've work to do in my office. I need to phone my managers with instructions to cover the next couple of months or more.'

She digested this information, then asked, 'Does that mean you're going away for a period of that length?'

'Have you forgotten that my vacation was interrupted?' he queried. 'It's still winter. I can still make up for lost time.'

So—he intends to go away, Judy thought as depression took a firm grip on her. That sure put paid to any intention of returning to Napier, she realised dejectedly, while staring through the alcove window at the grey-green waters of the bay.

Moments later she heard rather than saw Ryan leave the room and go downstairs. No word of forgiveness, she noticed, and began to suspect that he'd become reconciled only when she left his house.

CHAPTER NINE

JUDY had no idea how long she sat huddled in a heap of despair. She knew that her presumption in believing Ryan to be Robin's father had offended him deeply, and she regretted not having had more faith in him. When he'd said that love needed trust, had he meant that he felt her response to his kisses to be insincere? And had this lack of trust in him killed any feelings he might have had for her?

How could she have been such an idiot? Right from the beginning she should have told herself that in no way would he have ignored his son's existence—she should have been sure of it. But had she given him the benefit of the doubt? No, she had not. Mentally, she had continued to insult him. It had registered with him and he'd resented it bitterly. After all, who could blame him?

Her unhappiness increased while she contemplated Ryan's future attitude towards herself. While he didn't impress her as being a man who bore grudges, it was possible that he'd take time to get over the fact that she'd considered him to be a deserter of his own son.

So what should she do? Surely there was only one course for her to take. She must go home and endeavour to forget him. Her suitcase was already half packed, but she had no wish to complete it. A sudden aversion to doing so kept her glued to the chair, because she knew that the filled case would mean the beginning of the end of her association with Ryan. It would mean the time was near when she'd never see him again, and that thought was unbearable.

And then the memory of his kisses swept into her mind. It was strange to be kissed by a man who was so annoyed with her, Judy mused. And as she recalled the delight of

147

those kisses, the joy of being held against him, she was shaken by a tremor that stirred her emotions into a state of chaos. Had he *meant* those caresses—or had they been merely a forerunner of punishment to come? Perhaps he'd intended to lead her along the path of romance and then tell her he didn't want a woman who could think so badly of him.

A surge of restlessness gripped her, causing her to leave the chair to collect the coffee mugs and carry them to the kitchen. There was also lunch to think about, which was a blessing, because it steered her mind away from the harsh words dealt to her by Ryan. Food—the way to a man's heart being through his stomach, she recalled, while putting tablemats and cutlery in place. However, she knew it would take more than food to find her way to this man's heart.

She was still pondering over what they'd have for lunch when Ryan came up the stairs. At least the table was laid, so it looked as if a meal might be almost ready. She regarded him anxiously. Was he still annoyed with her? Then, with her mistake of believing him to be Robin's father still swirling in her mind, she said, 'Ryan, I do want to apologise...'

'Forget it,' he snapped tersely.

'I can't forget it and I want you to know I'm sorry...'

'I've no wish to discuss it,' he retorted. 'What's for lunch?'

'Mousetraps,' she said with sudden inspiration.

He glared at her. '*Mousetraps*...as in the things you catch mice with? I don't think I fancy them. Or is this supposed to be funny?'

'You're not thinking clearly,' she accused sharply. 'Surely you're not taking me *literally*...or are you?'

'Why not? You took me literally when I called Robin *son*. Besides, a man can never tell what ridiculous ideas women get into their heads.'

He's still feeling thoroughly cross, Judy realised, then

told herself to have patience. 'It's all right, I quite understand,' she said quietly, making a determined effort to prevent his words from getting to her. And before they could make her say something she'd regret she went on shakily, 'I've *tried* to say I'm sorry, but you won't listen, and now you're having trouble in controlling the fury that's got you in its grip.'

'Damned rubbish,' he snorted. 'I am not furious.'

A small laugh echoed her disbelief. 'No? You could've fooled me. I'd say it's been gnawing at you ever since you've been downstairs. Why don't you relax and read your Sunday paper? It hasn't even been opened.'

'You're right—I'll do that,' he agreed, shaking the paper open with more force than necessary.

'I'll attend to the mousetraps. They'll take only a few minutes,' she said with forced cheerfulness.

There was no reply as he settled himself in the chair he usually occupied. The paper rustled and he remained hidden behind its pages.

More depression descended upon Judy as she went to the kitchen, but she pushed it aside while placing two slices of bread in the toaster. When they popped up, nicely browned, they were set on an oval plate, then their outer crusts were edged with grated cheese to form a nest. An egg was broken into each hollow, and after the yolks and whites had been well pricked, each one was liberally sprinkled with bacon stock powder and extra grated cheese. A little more than a minute was all they needed in the microwave.

A moment later she carried the plate to the table, while saying with forced brightness, 'Bacon and egg mousetraps coming up.'

He lowered the paper and spoke gruffly. 'What...? Already...?'

'I told you it would take only a few minutes. Please don't allow it to go cold. I'll make your coffee—or would you rather have tea?'

He ignored the question by demanding, 'Where are your own "mousetraps"? Don't you intend to have lunch?'

'Not today, thank you. I don't feel like eating.'

His mouth tightened. 'Why not?'

She decided to be frank. 'Because unpleasantness at mealtimes usually upsets me. I'll go and...and continue packing my suitcase. It won't take long to complete the job.' Her voice held a slight tremor as she went on, 'After that I'll walk to the motel.'

'To the *motel*? What the hell for?' he rasped.

'To see if they have a vacancy, of course. I've no intention of staying in the house of a man who resents my presence to the extent that you obviously do,' she informed him, while taking a deep breath to calm herself.

He stared at her intently, then apparently decided that she meant what she said. His tone softened as he spoke quietly. 'You're not going anywhere. You'll make lunch for yourself, or I'll toss this lot into the rubbish bin—which would be a pity because they smell good. Bacon and cheese—who can resist it?' He inhaled deeply while savouring the appetising aroma.

She capitulated because she wanted to, but placed only one slice of bread in the toaster. A few minutes later she carried the plate to the table and sat opposite him. 'It was satisfactory?' she queried dryly, while observing his almost empty plate.

'You're a good cook,' he remarked with appreciation. 'I've noticed it before.'

She glowed inwardly, at the same time contemplating his earlier words. 'Why would you object to my going to the motel?' she asked, while finishing the food on her plate.

'Because I want you here.' It was a blunt statement.

She was amazed, but she kept her voice controlled as she said, 'Then you'd better understand that I have no intention of staying here if you're continually cross with me. I can't take the trauma of it, and I don't intend to try.' She paused for several moments, then went on pointedly, 'I recall you were mighty keen to put me in the motel when I first arrived. If it hadn't been for a certain small party's performance you'd have run me there right smartly.'

His eyes became hooded as he said enigmatically, 'Yes...well...things have happened since then. And I must confess I'm missing that same small party, even though he's only just left.'

'So am I,' Judy admitted dolefully.

'He's a fine little boy, although there are times when he needs discipline.' Ryan chuckled. 'I've a strong suspicion he's about to be introduced to it. Homework before riding Bluebell—that sort of thing.'

He's edging away from the subject, Judy realised, then made an attempt to drag him back to it. 'You still haven't told me why you want me to stay here,' she persisted.

He stared at his empty plate, as though expecting to find the answer there. 'Call it a whim,' he said at last. 'You said you'd like to find a job in Napier, and I'd like to see you do it. But in the meantime you must have somewhere to stay, and I see no reason for you to move out of this place. You can look upon it as a small token of gratitude for all the meals you prepared when Robin was here. You didn't come here expecting to take over as cook.'

Gratitude, she thought with disgust. Not even the smallest hint of wanting her company. Well, the sooner she became accustomed to the fact that he didn't want her for herself, the sooner she'd get over the nagging ache of longing to feel his arms holding her against him.

Almost as though reading her thoughts, and wishing to get away from them, he stood up abruptly and moved towards the kitchen. 'I'll make the coffee,' he muttered over his shoulder.

In a way it was a blessing, because it gave her a respite from the penetrating gaze that had been sending colour to her cheeks and causing her to feel self-conscious. And without his piercing scrutiny she was able to think a little more clearly. She was able to ask herself a question—if not for her company, why would he insist upon her staying here? *'Because I want you here'*, he'd said. It seemed very odd, considering her ability to annoy him.

And then the memory of something Ryan had said leapt into her mind—something that now caused her to sit slowly upright as she recalled his words. They'd been spoken just after he'd produced the tapestry that was to have served him as a reminder never to become involved with another woman. Cynthia's name and her 'plan' had crept into the conversation, and then Ryan had said, *'Maybe I have a plan of my own.'*

Her curiosity stirred, she pondered the question of asking him about it. But would she be wise to do so? Wouldn't she be laying herself open to receiving a well-deserved re-buff for being so inquisitive? After all, it was not her business, and no doubt he'd consider her to be again prying into his private affairs. And then the sight of his tanned, well-shaped hand placing coffee beside her shook her out of her contemplations.

'Your thoughts appear to have pushed you into a day-dream,' Ryan remarked. 'Care to share them, or are they too private for words?'

Judy looked down at her hands. She thought quickly, then returned to a former subject. 'I've been wondering about my future, and the possibility of finding a job in Christchurch.'

'Does this mean you've changed your mind about work-ing in Napier?' he demanded sharply.

'No. I mean, I haven't changed my mind about wanting to work in Napier...I just think it would be wiser not to stay in Napier, and especially in this house.'

He sent her a hard look. 'I'm sure you must be able to explain that reasoning. Why are you throwing my offer back in my face?' His voice had become like granite.

She sighed. 'There I go again—making you mad...'

'I'm waiting for an explanation.'

She took a deep breath. 'Very well. The offer was made

when we were out in the boat. Since then you've become really infuriated with me…I mean more infuriated than usual…but you're now making the offer again because you can't bear to go back on your word. It's a matter of your honour. Well, I'm not staying here under those circumstances.'

'OK—if that's the way you want it.' His tone was abrupt.

No persuasion to change her mind, she noticed, feeling swamped by disappointment. And then his next question surprised her.

'This business of believing I was Robin's father—did the dragon put the idea into your head?'

'In a way I suppose she did. She declared that you should've married Verna years ago, and there was also the fact that she'd sent the boy to you. I thought it added up to only one solution.' Judy looked at him anxiously. 'Please try to understand how it became stuck in my mind, especially with help from *you*.'

'OK, I can see your point,' he conceded gruffly. 'And now that you're aware of the truth can we drop the subject?'

'Only if you'll say you forgive me.' Somehow she had to hear him say the words that meant he was no longer holding it against her. Then, as he merely looked at her in thoughtful silence, Judy's chin rose and she added scathingly, 'Please don't strain yourself in trying to do so. I'll quite understand.'

Ryan appeared to pull himself together. 'Of course I forgive you,' he muttered huskily. 'How could you doubt it?'

'Very easily,' she retorted, then breathed a sigh of relief. The fear of Ryan's continued resentment had been enough to make her feel thoroughly miserable. She longed for him to take her in his arms and kiss her better, but he made no move to do so. Couldn't he see she was feeling low? she wondered. Obviously he couldn't care less.

'You'll unpack your suitcase?' he queried casually.

'Only when I know your real reason for wishing me to stay here,' she returned with stubborn determination.

Again he regarded her in silence, and as though considering the matter, then he grinned, while speaking in a nonchalant manner. 'Actually, there are several reasons. Let's just say I've become accustomed to having you about the place. My home would seem empty without you.'

'Would it, indeed?' She found his words to be of little comfort. He was being deliberately flippant, therefore she replied in a similar vein. 'Are you trying to say you'd actually miss me?'

'Something like that,' he admitted offhandedly. 'Also, I rather like seeing your face at the breakfast table. In winter it brightens a dull morning.'

'Thank you…you're too kind.' He's only joking, she told herself, but was unable to resist asking, 'What are the other reasons? You said there were several.'

He rubbed his chin reflectively as he said, 'I like to hear you moving about the house. There's a huge difference between you and Kate.'

'You don't say!' she retorted, while beginning to feel slightly irritated.

'I do indeed. If it came to a choice I'd choose you any day.' He spoke gravely but Judy caught a twinkle in his olive-green eyes.

She began to feel frustrated, realising she'd get little sense out of him. However, she remained calm as she said, 'Thank you again…I'm overwhelmed with gratitude.'

He went on, 'And there's the way you keep flowers in the house. The bowls of polyanthus and pansies make such a difference. Kate never bothers about them. She doesn't give the place a feminine touch, whereas you…you bring it to life.'

She looked at him doubtfully, searching for a hint of mockery in his words. Better not take him seriously, she decided, then spoke dryly. 'Your kind words are going to my head. It's a pity you don't mean even a few of them.'

'I'm not in the habit of making statements I don't mean,' he reminded her coolly. 'You asked for reasons, and I've offered you a few of them. Haven't they told you *anything*?'

'Only a very little. Not the real reason…' She bit her lip and fell silent just in time.

'Not the reason you wanted to hear?' he queried softly, his eyes taking on the penetrating gleam with which she was becoming familiar.

'Let's just say they've failed to give sufficient reason for me to unpack my suitcase,' she prevaricated brightly. If he could be trifling about these matters, so could she. It was a game that two could play. And then a stirring of memory caused her to say, 'But shouldn't you be packing your own suitcase? Didn't you say you intend to take the vacation that was interrupted when Robin and I arrived?'

'Yes, but my plans for it are not yet complete,' he said dismissively, and as though having no wish to be questioned about it.

'Is it part of your *own* plan that you once mentioned?' curiosity forced her to ask.

'I'll admit there's a connection,' he confessed with a grin, then rose to his feet abruptly, adding, 'I must go to my office and check on the moon.'

'The *moon*?' She looked at him uncomprehendingly. 'In broad daylight?'

'No, on the calendar—for seed-planting time. The moon affects more than the tides, you know. Seeds for a root crop do better if planted when a waning moon drags them down, while seeds for a top crop should be drawn up by a waxing moon. Didn't I tell you there's a season for everything?'

'Is there a season for love?' she asked, before she could stop the words passing her lips, then felt irritated by the colour she knew to be creeping into her cheeks.

'Only for those who trust and have faith in each other,' he told her in a matter-of-fact tone, then went towards the stairs, where he paused to turn and look at her. 'I'll probably be downstairs for the rest of the afternoon. There's always plenty to do before one goes away. You'll be able to amuse yourself?'

She nodded without speaking as, frustrated, she watched him disappear down the stairs without a backward glance. *'Only for those who trust and have faith in each other'*, he'd said. Was that his way of telling her she'd failed to qualify? OK—she'd got the message.

And then the knowledge that she'd been pushed aside gripped her with painful force. And she was also hit by the fact that his attitude towards her had changed. Previously, and despite Robin's presence in the house, Ryan had often taken her in his arms. He'd kissed and held her against him in an embrace that had been warm and vibrant, filling her with quivering desire. But now that they had the house to themselves, and were without fear of interruption from a small boy, had there been so much as a touching of hands? No, there had not.

Judy turned towards the window and stared sightlessly at the hills across the bay. Again she realised she was being given a message—one that was coming through loud and clear. This relationship was to be kept on an even keel and without emotion of any kind. Ryan appeared to be saying that without so much as uttering the words.

The knowledge filled her with a sadness that made her want to weep, but she was determined to avoid tears. Instead, she directed her mind towards a more positive line of thought, and it was Robin's face that sprang into her vision. His shining eyes and broad smile beaming from the car as it was driven away had indicated the happiest of boys. He had his mum and his dad—and his pony. What more could he ask for? Perhaps someone to tidy the room he'd left, Judy thought as she went towards it.

It took only a short time to change the sheets and remake the bed, then Judy went to her own room, where her half-filled suitcase lay open and gaping at her from the floor.

Go on—fill me and get the job done, it seemed to say. *There's no room for you in this house.*

The last thought was enough to make her take a few more undies from the drawers, and as she tucked them neatly into the case a sound caught her ears. She looked up to discover Ryan watching her from the doorway. The sight of his athletic form and handsome face made her heart turn over, but she merely said, 'You've finished in the office already?'

He gave a rueful grin. 'I've hardly scratched the surface. I've come up to tell you not to prepare a meal this evening. I'm taking you out to dinner.'

'You are…?' Her blue eyes widened as her lovely face glowed with happy surprise. 'Thank you… I…I don't know what to say.'

'No need to say anything. Why should it be such a shock?'

'Because…I didn't come here expecting entertainment or…or to be taken out to dinner,' she returned quietly. 'Besides, we couldn't have gone out and left a small boy in the house.'

'Of course not. However, I've been more than aware that you've had a dull time here. At one stage I wondered about asking Kate to babysit Robin, then I decided against it. If he'd woken up and she'd appeared in his room all hell would have been let loose.'

'You're probably right about *that*, but you're not correct in thinking I've had a dull time here. I've enjoyed living here. I can understand Cynthia being keen to move in.'

'You can, huh?' He sent her a hard stare, then changed the subject by saying, 'I see you've almost finished packing.'

'Yes…I was about to fold dresses into it.'

'Good,' he said succinctly. Then he left her.

The word stabbed at her. It was *good* to see that she'd packed her case in readiness to leave? If her lack of faith in his integrity still bugged him, why was he taking her out this evening? But she refused to ponder the question, and in a whirl of excitement she went to the wardrobe to decide upon what to wear.

Flinging the door open, she breathed a sigh of relief as her eyes rested upon a gentian-blue dress she'd almost forgotten she'd brought with her. Made of fine wool, and designed with long sleeves, it had a matching jacket that enabled it to be worn in winter, and with it she would wear the sapphires that had belonged to her great-grandmother. The earrings peeped through her blonde hair, while the ornately set pendant nestled against the cleavage revealed by the low V-neck of the dress.

Judy had protested when her mother had suggested packing the blue dress. 'For heaven's sake, Mother, I'll never wear it,' she'd declared. 'Mrs Simmons expects me to return the next day.'

'Forget Mrs Simmons,' her mother had advised acidly. 'I can guess why *she* wants you away from that man. But you never know what happens to alter arrangements, and I have a strong feeling you'll be there for longer than overnight. If I were you I'd take enough clothing for a week or more. There's nothing like being prepared for the unexpected.'

And now Judy was thankful she'd followed her mother's advice. As things had turned out she had not only needed the extra clothes, but was now relieved she would be able to step into the blue dress.

Later, as she entered the living room, her recently washed hair gleaming like a halo against the intense blue, Ryan stood up slowly. There was a silence for several long moments as he stood staring at her, then he strode across the room and took her small hands in a firm grip. 'You look wonderful,' his deep voice murmured huskily.

'Thank you.' His words sent a flush to her cheeks, and for one mad moment she imagined he intended to kiss her. When he made no move to do so she raked her mind for something with which to reciprocate. 'Have you ever realised that evening clothes make a man look…quite hand-some?' she queried almost teasingly as he released her hands.

'You reckon I'll pass with a push?' he asked in a dry tone.

She nodded without speaking. 'Quite handsome' had been a colossal understatement. The words that had actually sprung into her mind had revolved round such terms as 'devastatingly impressive', or 'spellbinding'—but to have uttered them would have been going over the top. He might have laughed at her, or, worse still, guessed that she loved him.

'Let's go.' He took her arm and led her towards the stairs with an air of possession. As they descended he reached to clasp her hand. His grip on her fingers sent the usual tremor through her. It also raised her spirits, making her hope he was no longer angry with her. Was it possible for this to be a dream evening? she wondered, while offering a small prayer that nothing would happen to ruin it.

They drove past the Port, where lights blazed on men working the container ships, then followed the coastal road into the city. Ryan led her into a restaurant on The Parade, and as their table was beside a window she found herself once more gazing up at the kaleidoscope of coloured lights laced through the branches of the lofty Norfolk pines.

The setting was romantic, she decided, while turning to watch the moonlight throw a silvery sparkle over this south-ern corner of the Pacific Ocean. Romantic—without a ves-tige of romance. Because, although he'd brought her out this evening, it was merely part of the gratitude he'd men-tioned. Beneath it resentment still simmered.

As if to contradict her thoughts, Ryan leaned across the table to murmur, 'I suppose you're aware that every man in the restaurant is shooting glances towards you?'

'You're exaggerating,' she returned lightly, then warned herself against allowing his compliment to send her off balance.

And then menus and a wine list were left for them to study. Ryan glanced at the former and made a rapid decision. 'Crab and mango as a starter, followed by veal cordon bleu with ham and Swiss cheese,' he said without hesitation.

Judy looked at him across the top of the printed page. 'You sound as though you know those dishes well.'

'I do. When I have guests I always bring them here.'

A guest. Of course, that was all she was, and she'd be wise to remember it. However, all she said was, 'I'll join you with the crab and mango, and the veal too.'

'I think you'll enjoy it,' he said, then ordered a bottle of rosé to complement the veal.

His use of the word 'guest' continued to niggle at her. Had it been a deliberate reminder that she was just a temporary visitor in his house? Or was her one-sided love for him sending her into a state of paranoia? Determined to push it aside and to display a cheerful front, she smiled as she said, 'You must have got your office work under control, otherwise you wouldn't have come out this evening.'

'Well, there are various things that Craig can handle for me. I'll take them to him tomorrow morning.'

'Craig? Is he one of your field managers?'

'No, he's Craig Birch—my accountant. He's also Cynthia's ex-husband. Craig and I go back a long way. Needless to say I met Cynthia through him. He's a decent man. She was a fool to leave him.'

'Oh?' She tried to sound uninterested.

Ryan went on, 'It was Craig who asked me to keep an eye on her investments. He knew jolly well that she wouldn't go to him for advice.'

'That was good of him, considering they're divorced,' Judy said.

Ryan frowned. 'I don't think he's ever lost his affection for her. I suspect he'd take her back tomorrow—if she'd go to him.'

'Does he know of her plan to move in with you?' Judy was unable to resist the question.

'Apparently she explained it at length. He warned me she'd be arriving the moment you'd vacated the premises. I told him you'd be gone by tomorrow.' His words were completely emotionless.

'Tomorrow.' Judy swallowed her food with difficulty, while trying to avoid looking as dismal as she felt. Obviously he didn't care a hoot that she'd be leaving tomorrow. And then his next words surprised her.

'After I'd told Craig about the plan I have in mind I realised I should also give a few more details of it to my managers, especially as I'll be away for longer than usual. So I arranged a meeting in my office for tomorrow morning. Do you think we can have date scones?'

'Yes, of course. But what time do I have to be at the airport?'

'Not until the next day. I changed our flight to Tuesday.'

'*Our* flight...?' She was beginning to feel confused.

He spoke casually. 'It's time I visited my packing suppliers in Christchurch, to see what new ideas they have. Maybe you'll introduce me to your parents. Anyone who stands up to the dragon has my deepest respect.'

'So, I *don't* leave tomorrow...' She felt as if she'd been given a reprieve. It was betrayed by the long breath that escaped her.

He stared at her intently. 'You sound almost...relieved.'

She returned his gaze squarely. 'I told you I've enjoyed being here—at least I have apart from the last few hours, when I've realised I hurt you so deeply. However, the point I'm unable to understand is why my thoughts concerning the matter should upset you to such an extent.'

'You can't, huh?' His mouth twisted slightly. 'You can't think of any reason why your lack of faith should send me up the wall or make me go berserk?'

She shook her head, then asked in a hushed voice, 'It was as bad as that? I'm sorry. Believe me, I'll never doubt you again—not that there'll be any opportunity to do so,' she added dolefully.

'Is that a promise?'

She nodded vigorously, then made an attempt to find a more cheerful subject by asking, 'Where do you intend to spend your main vacation? I can't imagine you'll stay in Christchurch for long.'

'You're right. After I've had a session with the packaging people there'll be little to hold me in Christchurch.'

His words came like a slap in the face to Judy, but she gave no sign of the pain they caused. After all, what else could she expect?

Ryan went on nonchalantly, 'When I've finished in Christchurch I'll take a flight to Singapore. Have you ever been there?'

'No. I...I'm afraid I've never been out of New Zealand.' She felt the admission made her look pathetic.

He went on to tell her about clean, well-ordered Singapore, with its variety of colourful orchids and numerous tourist attractions. He'd been there once, and was now looking forward to a return visit.

Judy's expression became wistful as she listened to Ryan's vivid description of Singapore, and, although she was interested in all the Asian island had to offer, her mind kept darting to the problem of being able to keep in contact with this man who held her heart. The thought of never seeing him again became more unthinkable every moment, but her pride would not allow him to become aware of it.

Nor was there much comfort when she recalled that he'd said she could remain in his house while seeking a job in Napier. He hadn't shown a great deal of enthusiasm about the idea—and there'd been no pleading for her to do so. He'd merely been offering a helping hand. And, despite the fact that he'd kissed her, he'd never uttered a single word of love or shown the slightest sign of commitment.

Suddenly an abrupt silence fell between them, and Ryan stared at her suspiciously. 'You've been gazing into space for the last several minutes,' he accused. 'I doubt that you've heard a word that I've said.'

She made an effort to pull her thoughts together, and to look as if she really had been listening. 'It all sounds wonderful,' she said.

'Then what put that trance-like look into your eyes?' he demanded. 'You looked almost sad.'

'Well, it is sad to think of you visiting those places alone. Most things are so much better when they're shared.'

'I quite agree. It's something I've learnt fairly recently.' He regarded her thoughtfully before asking, 'What makes you so sure I'll be taking this Singapore trip alone?'

'Only the fact that you haven't told me about a companion going with you.' She hesitated, then asked, 'Are you saying you *will* have somebody with you?'

'I'm hoping so. Actually, I haven't asked her yet.'

Her? The word came as a shock. He must mean Cynthia, she thought, while misery engulfed her like a black cloud and jealousy began to rage within her. Yet why should she be so surprised? She had never been able to guess at his true feelings for Cynthia because his natural reserve kept them hidden.

Dared she ask the question that kept jabbing at her mind? An answer would at least give her an indication of his feelings towards Cynthia. That was if he'd tell her, of course. Or would he point out that it was not her concern? Hesitatingly she queried in a small voice, 'You're hoping to take Cynthia with you?'

The moment the words were out she knew she'd made a mistake. The look on his face confirmed it, especially when she saw his mouth harden into a thin line, and watched his expression become bleak.

'I thought you promised not to do that again,' he said, in a flat, dull tone that betrayed barely concealed irritation.

'D-do wh-what...?' she stammered, feeling slightly bewildered.

'Put me into the class of being a two-faced rat.'

'I...I don't understand,' she protested. 'How did I do that?'

'By pulling my integrity to pieces—just as you did over Robin. Didn't I tell you that Craig and I go back a long way? He's not only my accountant; he's also my *friend*. Didn't I tell you he'd have Cynthia back tomorrow if she'd go to him? No way would I take the woman he still loves to Singapore.'

Judy felt not only stricken by remorse, but also infuriated by her own stupidity. She recalled offering a small prayer that nothing would happen to ruin this evening, and now, while nothing tangible had occurred to spoil it, she herself had been successful in doing so by asking that idiotic question. Nor was it possible to explain that jealousy had clouded her thinking.

'I'm sorry,' she mumbled, while pushing the remains of her dessert a few inches from her.

Ryan made no reply. He merely signalled for the bill.

CHAPTER TEN

JUDY was frustrated during the drive home. She'd done it again—she'd really annoyed him. And now she realised the importance of exonerating herself, by giving reasons for the thoughtless question that had made Ryan so irate.

As they drove round the seafront she took several deep breaths to control the tremor she feared would be in her voice, then, despite the grimness of his handsome profile, she took courage and said in a slightly defiant tone, 'I know you're mad with me again, but I had no idea there was any depth of friendship between you and Cynthia's ex-husband. Apart from this evening you haven't even mentioned his name—so how was I to know?' The last words came plaintively.

'Hadn't I just told you that Craig and I go back a long way?'

'Yes, but that doesn't mean...'

'I presumed you'd *understand* there was friendship between us.' He paused, then went on reflectively, 'I suppose the question of my friends hasn't really arisen. I'm looked upon as a hermit without any—remember?'

'Obviously that's not correct,' Judy said. 'According to Cynthia you and she are *very close*. So close, in fact, that she plans to move in with you...and you yourself told me *that*.' Her tone almost betrayed her jealousy.

'I merely told you what *she* thinks,' Ryan retorted harshly. He scowled at the road ahead. 'Personally, I've never believed she's been serious about it, otherwise I'd have told her to forget the idea.'

'She sounded very serious to me,' Judy informed him quietly.

165

'Then she's daft,' he snorted. 'She *knows* Craig is my friend. She couldn't possibly expect me to take her in, especially when her own parents live in Napier. If she wants to live in this city she can go to them.'

Judy spoke in a low, tense voice. 'Ryan, I think you're underrating her determination. When I recall all she has said to me I feel sure she has every intention of moving in with you. Didn't she ask Kate to let her know when the house is free of...guests?'

'Yes, well...'

'And didn't you say she'd told Craig she'd be moving in the moment I'd gone?' Judy reminded him.

'That was her way of hurting him—and, as I've already pointed out, she knows he's my friend,' Ryan said, as though that settled the matter.

But Judy was not convinced. Turning to regard Ryan, she spoke earnestly. 'I think she feels it's a matter of all being fair in love and war. It's also possible she believes that what she has to offer will override any scruples you may have about friendship.' A flush had risen to Judy's cheeks as she'd forced herself to utter these last words.

'In that case she'll be making a mistake,' Ryan said tersely.

'So, what shall you do when she turns up at your door with her suitcase?'

He shrugged. 'I've no idea. I'll cross that war zone when—and if ever—I come to it,' he returned easily.

By the time they reached home Judy was feeling more cheerful. And, although she suspected that Ryan was still annoyed with her, she at least knew he was not in love with Cynthia. Which was something she'd secretly feared. Not that it made much difference, because neither was he in love with herself.

Nor did she believe he was as unaware of Cynthia's intentions as he'd appeared to be. No doubt this fact was his real reason for suggesting that she should stay in his house while seeking a job in Napier. It wasn't because he wanted her company, Judy thought sadly. It was merely a ploy to prevent Cynthia from making an attempt to move in.

She stepped from the garage to the hall, and these thoughts were abruptly swept from her mind by the sight of diffused light at the top of the stairs. A sudden fear gripped her. Had Cynthia arrived even before her own departure? Had she procured the key from Kate during their absence? She glanced at Ryan. 'Did we leave lights on upstairs?' she asked nervously.

He grinned. 'No, but now you'll see my cave when it's been burnished by elves with pots of gold,' he said teasingly, and without switching on the stair light he took her hand and led her up through the gloom.

On the landing she stood almost mesmerised while gazing at the golden light flooding the living room and dining alcove. The area had been transformed into a place of mystery and intrigue, and it was caused by the street lamps, which sent an amber glow through the windows. Late sunshine shooting through autumn leaves, she thought.

'Do you find it eerie?' Ryan asked.

Judy's eyes moved from the almost yellow highlights to the depth of shadows. 'Not at all. I find it quite fascinating—even romantic.' Then she went on hastily, 'Why haven't I seen it like this before?'

'Because the lights have always been on and the curtains drawn.'

His showing her the rooms in this aureate state made her feel that perhaps he was no longer quite so annoyed with her, and she wished to thank him for taking her out. 'Thank you for a lovely evening, Ryan,' she said. 'It's one I'll remember.'

'Because the food was good—or because the host bit your head off?'

'I...I suppose I deserved it,' she admitted. 'I seem to be good at saying stupid things. Please forgive me.' Impulsively, she stood on tiptoe and kissed his cheek.

Her action brought a quick response. Still standing in the

golden glow, he snatched her to him, and, hugging her closely, he kissed her brow, her cheeks and her lips, where his mouth lingered for several long moments. His hands found their way down her spine to clasp her even closer, but although she clung to him, with her heart thudding, they moved to her shoulders then put her away from him with gentle firmness.

Looking down into her face, he spoke huskily. 'Shall we start again—back to square one?'

Hesitantly, she asked, 'Where, exactly, was square one?'

'That was the afternoon you arrived. I was knocked sideways by your determination to care for Robin.'

'Knocked. sideways...?' His words amazed her. 'I thought your main aim was to be rid of me.'

'Well, I no longer wish to be rid of you.'

The light in the room made everything seem unreal. Had she actually heard those words? They made her heart sing, but she said nothing while waiting for more—such as the fact that she meant something deeper to him. However, such a statement did not come.

Instead he switched on the living-room lights and the golden mystique disappeared in a flash. Everything was back to normal, especially when he said, 'I must go to my office and tidy a few odds and ends that should've been attended to this evening. See you in the morning. Don't forget the date scones.'

Date scones. Frustration made her fume inwardly. Why on earth had she fallen in love with this man? Because he had so many attributes to love, she realised. Apart from his generosity and kindness, there was his thoughtfulness. Even his reason for wishing to meet her parents had stirred her gratitude. 'If you're to stay with me while looking for a job in Napier, don't you think they'd like to look me over?' he'd said, when the subject had come up again. She knew there would never be anyone else for her. Ryan was the only man she'd ever love.

As for the person he might be taking to Singapore—

could it be an aunt or a cousin? Surely he had such relatives. She put the question away from her, refusing to even think about it. Instead, she decided to just live for today, and the short time she would have left with him in Christchurch.

Later, as she lay in her bed, Judy became aware of a deep longing. She imagined she could still feel the strength of Ryan's arms crushing her against his body, and the pressure of his lips on her own. Could it be the same with him? she wondered wistfully. Was it possible the memory would bring him to her room? A small groan escaped her as she ached to lie in his arms.

Turning her head, she stared at the bedroom door. Normally she closed it, but tonight she'd left it ajar. Would he recognise it as a message that she was waiting for him? Tension gripped her as she lay listening for him to come upstairs, and it seemed ages before she heard sounds that indicated he'd gone to the kitchen.

Impulsively, she sprang out of bed, threw on her wrap and stepped into slippers. Her hair in a blonde tangle, she went to the kitchen, where she found him heating milk. 'You needed a hot drink?' she queried from beneath the archway.

He turned to stare at her, then removed the beaker from the microwave. 'Hot milk at night helps me to sleep,' he said. 'Would you like to join me?'

Suddenly conscious of her dishevelled appearance, she clutched her wrap more tightly about her. And then the fear that she might betray her yearning to be near him made her say, 'No, thank you. I...I just thought I could make a hot drink for you.'

'That was sweet of you. Thank you, but it's all under control.'

'Then I'll go back to bed...' She turned to leave, but before she'd taken more than a couple of steps he was beside her.

Sweeping her up into his arms, he cradled her like a

child. 'Allow me to help you on your way,' he said, while grinning down into her face, then he strode towards the bedroom.

A small gasp escaped Judy as wild hope surged through her. And as her heart began to hammer she flung her arms round Ryan's neck. Somewhere along the passage she felt her slippers fall off, but the fact barely registered.

At her bedside he untied the girdle of her wrap, then slipped the garment from her shoulders. The nightdress she wore was long-sleeved, and of winter weight, but did nothing to conceal the rounded mounds of her breasts beneath it. His eyes rested upon them briefly before he took her in his arms and kissed her deeply.

Her entire being leapt to respond, and as she clung to him her need to be loved forced an involuntary arch towards him, calling as plainly as if she'd spoken the words.

A low groan escaped him. His arms tightened about her, then his hands went to her buttocks, pulling her towards him—until suddenly he froze. His hands moved to draw her arms from about his neck, and, sweeping her up to cradle her again, he deposited her on the bed. He drew the blankets over her, and his deep voice spoke huskily. 'Tomorrow…it'll be a big day tomorrow…'

She gaped at him, her hopes crashing about her. 'Tomorrow? What's so special about tomorrow?'

But he'd gone, closing the door behind him.

Staring at the closed door, Judy felt both humiliated and rejected. Ryan *knew* she'd wanted to make love. She'd been too obvious for words. And no doubt he'd guessed she was hopelessly in love with him. But he'd been kind to her about it. He'd kissed her and held her close—and then he'd said *no*, as gently as he could. Not in a word, but by his actions. Mortified, she lay back, pulled the blankets over her head, and cursed herself for having gone to the kitchen.

'OK, Ryan—message received,' she mumbled in a state of misery, and the tears fell and muffled sobs began to shake her body.

*   *   *

Next morning Judy hoped she didn't look as dismal as she felt. Sleep had eluded her during the night, and she had spent the hours of darkness in trying to come to terms with the fact that Ryan did not love her. At least, not in the way that she loved him, or in the way that she *wanted* to be loved. He did not even seem to want her any more.

Granted, he liked her company, and she knew he thought she was easy on the eye. He'd also been kind enough to offer her accommodation while she searched for a job in Napier, but that was as far as it went, and she had no option but to become accustomed to the situation.

Despite the depression engulfing her, she took care to put on a cheerful face at the breakfast table when she asked, 'What time is your meeting? I mean…at what time would you like the scones to be ready?'

'The men will be here by nine-thirty,' he told her. 'We'll have coffee at ten-thirty. Normally I serve it with biscuits in the office, but this time it's a little more special, so I'll bring them up to the dining alcove. The scones won't be too much trouble?'

'Of course not,' she assured him hastily. 'I'll be pleased to make them for you.' Which was true. She'd do anything for him.

'Thank you. There'll be six of us.'

'Why is this a special meeting?' she queried.

He thought for several moments before he said, 'It's the beginning of a new season. I told you that everything has its season—remember?'

'Yes, I remember.' Except for a season for love, she recalled, leaving the words unspoken.

He went on, 'A new season is like the opening of a new life. It's always special. This one happens to be much more special than any others.' His eyes held her gaze as he uttered the last words.

'Why is that? Or should I be minding my own business?'

He grinned at her. 'Just bear with me until this evening and I'll tell you all about it. I need to have a clear head to check that I've covered the long list of things that must be attended to.'

She looked at him wonderingly. 'I don't understand. You've said you'll be away for a longer period than usual...but...are you saying that by telling me you *won't* have a clear head?'

'It's more than possible,' he admitted. 'I'm not accustomed to being up in the air—' He broke off, as though having said too much, then stood up abruptly. 'See you later,' he said, striding towards the stairs.

Sensing the subdued exhilaration Ryan appeared to be keeping under control, Judy wished a little of it could be rubbed off on herself. Wearily, she left the table and attended to the breakfast dishes, and a short time later became busy with her baking. At least it gave her something to think about.

She had just tipped the scone mixture from the bowl to the worktop when Ryan entered the kitchen unheard.

A sharp gasp escaped her as his arms encircled her from behind, his hands resting gently on her waist. 'Do you want to get flour everywhere?'

'I'll tell the men I've been kissing the cook,' he murmured against her ear. 'I trust all the right ingredients have gone into the mixture? We don't want bricks to be served.'

Quivering from the sensations shooting through her, she said, 'If you don't remove your hands *nothing* will be served.'

'OK! OK! I was just checking to make sure all is well with you. I thought you looked rather pale and wan during breakfast. I wouldn't like the men to get the idea I've been tying you to the kitchen sink,' he added lightly.

Judy laughed as she said innocently, 'Oh, they're unlikely to think that. Doesn't that only happen to wives or housekeepers? You already have the latter—and, as to the former, I'm sure your men know of your extreme allergy towards the marital state.'

'Yes, well...I've been thinking about that...' But before

he could say more the sound of the front doorbell floated up the stairs.

'Thinking what?' she asked, more eagerly than she'd intended.

'We'll discuss it this evening,' he said, then left her to answer the doorbell.

This evening? Would he discuss it then—or would the issue be dodged? she wondered. Why was he blowing hot one minute and cold the next? Depression bearing down upon her, she completed the scones, then went to her room. Pale and wan, he'd said. Peering at herself in the mirror, she decided she'd better do something about her face. And perhaps her gold skirt and top would enable her to look less like a load of misery.

Later, when the men came upstairs, she was feeling more cheerful—which was just as well, because intuition told her they were examining her critically. However, she smiled as she coped with their jocular remarks about it being the first time they'd been treated to the feminine touch, and that it was high time Ryan had a woman in the house.

But more dejection set in when the men left, because Ryan left with them. 'Don't expect me home for lunch,' he said. 'I'll have it with Craig, and then I have some shopping to do. I'll see you later in the afternoon. You'll be OK?'

'Of course.' Judy smiled to hide her disappointment as she went on, 'Please don't worry about me. I'll finish my packing, and I'll also go next door to say goodbye to Miss Coster.'

He nodded his approval. 'Good. She'll be pleased you've taken the trouble to do so. Shall you tell her you're thinking about seeking a job in Napier?'

Judy hesitated, then admitted, 'No. I...I haven't quite made up my mind about that yet. I...I can't help wondering if it would be wiser for me to...to stay away from this place.' Did he realise why? she wondered, watching his face anxiously.

'It's for you to decide,' he retorted in a cool tone, then turned and followed the men down the stairs.

Was that all he could say by way of persuasion? she asked herself gloomily. *Fool.* Now was not the time—even if he had *any* intention of doing so.

Moments later she was straining her ears to hear the opening and closing of the garage door. But Ryan had been busy with an oil can, and the sound of squeaks no longer came up the stairs. It made her feel that even the echoes of his arrival and departure were being denied her. As for the door itself—it was like a barrier that shut her out of his life. You're being a whimsical idiot, she told herself.

It was mid-afternoon when Judy went to the neighbouring cottage. Kate insisted upon making tea, and they chatted amicably. The visit was short, and as Judy was leaving the older woman spoke sincerely.

'I'm sorry you're going away. Ryan needs someone like you. I'd rather see him with you than with that woman from Te Pohue. You don't try to remind me that I'm just the *cleaning woman.*'

Judy smiled at her. 'That's because I don't *think* of you as a cleaning woman, Miss Coster. To me you are a retired school teacher who has been most helpful to Ryan.'

Kate beamed at her. 'Thank you, my dear. I hope I'll see you again some day. Is there any chance that you and Ryan...?'

Judy gave a shaky laugh. 'Not a hope in Hades. You know his feelings about having a woman in the house.' Impulsively, she gave Kate a hug, then hastened home to finish packing her suitcase.

She was folding the gentian-blue dress when she heard the front doorbell. It couldn't be Ryan, she thought, straightening her back. He'd drive in through the garage. Perhaps it was a hawker, with something to sell. She ran downstairs, opened the front door, and found herself faced by Cynthia Birch. On the mat beside the tall redhead was a large suitcase.

Cynthia's jaw sagged as she glared at Judy in amazement. *'You...you're still here...'* she burst out furiously.

'Of course I'm still here.' Despite her own warning to Ryan, Cynthia's actual arrival had given Judy a shock.

'I was told you'd be leaving for Christchurch on today's early plane,' Cynthia declared in an exasperated tone. 'Craig said that Ryan had told him so.'

'That was the plan—until Ryan changed his mind about leaving today,' Judy informed her. 'This morning he had a meeting with his managers—which means we shall not be leaving until tomorrow's plane.' The thought caused her to smile happily.

Cynthia's eyes narrowed. She drew a deep breath as she demanded, *'We... What are you talking about? What do you mean by we?'*

Judy's smile broadened. 'Ryan is coming to Christchurch with me.'

'You're lying,' Cynthia spat.

'I'm not. He'd like to meet my parents. You've only to ask him.'

'You can bet I'll do just that,' Cynthia hooted, with a fresh burst of fury.

'I'm afraid he's not here at the moment...'

'So you say. Get out of my way...I'll find him myself.' She pushed past Judy, lugging her suitcase into the hall and dumping it near the office door. 'I'll leave it there,' she panted. 'Ryan will carry it up for me.' Then she called to him while ascending the stairs. 'Ryan...where are you? It's me...Cynthia...'

Judy sped after her. 'I'm telling you...*he's not here.* Look in the garage—you'll see the Range Rover isn't there.'

Cynthia ignored her, moving rapidly from one room to another in search of Ryan. When she came to his bedroom she stood clasping her hands while gazing about her in a state of ecstasy. 'I'll love sleeping in here,' she exclaimed joyously. 'I've always wanted a room with a sea view—and this one's fantastic.'

'You've no right to be in this room.' Judy's voice rose to a higher pitch as it shook with anger. She glanced at her watch. Where was Ryan? Why was he taking so long to come home?

Cynthia regarded her loftily. 'You're pathetic. Of course I have every right to be in here. I know Ryan wants me to move in with him. He's proved it by the way he's taken care of my finances. He's got over his determination to keep women out of his house. You yourself paved the way for me—you and that child…'

Exasperated, Judy spoke vehemently. 'You're making a mistake, Cynthia. Ryan has integrity. He's Craig's *friend. That's* why he won't allow you to move in with him.'

'Nonsense. You don't know a thing about it,' Cynthia's words were sneered scornfully.

'I know what he's *told* me,' Judy flung at her.

'You're lying,' Cynthia shrieked at her. Then she gave a derisive laugh. 'In any case, he won't give Craig a second thought when he's in bed with me.' As though to drive the point home, she moved towards the bed and lay on it, stretching herself like a cat basking in the sun. 'It'll be wonderful,' she gloated. 'I just can't wait.'

The sight of Cynthia on Ryan's bed was too much for Judy—and then the thought of her *in the bed* made her see red. Her temper bubbled over and slipped from her control, and, scarcely knowing what she was doing, she rushed into his *en suite* bathroom in search of something to hold water.

An ornamental jug on the windowsill caught her eye. She filled it and returned to the bedroom, grim purpose oozing from every pore. Glaring at Cynthia, she spat, 'Get off that bed—or you'll get the lot…'

Startled, Cynthia sat up. 'You wouldn't dare…'

'Try me and see…'

Instinct seemed to warn Cynthia that Judy meant what

she said. She leapt from the bed and almost ran from the room.

Judy replaced the jug in the bathroom, and, her face white and set, followed the other woman into the living room.

Cynthia turned to face her. 'Look, Judy, you might as well simmer down and make up your mind to the situation. Why don't you finish packing that suitcase I saw on your bedroom floor? Ryan will probably book you in at the motel tonight.'

'He's unlikely to do that,' Judy snapped.

'Oh, yes, he will. He'll do it because I'm here. Don't you understand? He'll do it because we don't want our style cramped by a third party in the house—especially tonight.'

Judy shook her head. She was beginning to feel drained. 'You've got it all wrong, Cynthia. Ryan's friendship with Craig means more to him than you realise. If he took you to bed he wouldn't be able to look Craig in the eye. He's too reliable and honest to doublecross a friend.'

'That's utter rubbish,' Cynthia scoffed. 'You poor innocent—you obviously don't know men.'

'I reckon I know this one,' Judy flared at her. 'I'll admit there was a time when I *didn't* know him—but now I trust him implicitly. I have a world of faith in him, and never again would I doubt his word. In fact I'd...I'd follow him to the ends of the earth—!' She stopped, appalled by the words that were slipping off her tongue. She'd had no intention of making these admissions to Cynthia, but somehow the woman had stirred her into such agitation she hardly knew what she was saying.

'Anyone would imagine you were in love with him,' Cynthia jeered.

Judy felt too exhausted to argue or deny the fact. 'Yes, I am—if you must know the truth. I love him very dearly. I shall always love him.'

Cynthia's tone became waspish. 'Then you'll have to learn to keep your claws off him—do you understand?'

Her words were cut short as they heard the sound of whistling coming from downstairs, and then Ryan's voice floated up to them. 'I'm home—*darling*.'

Cynthia swept a triumphant glance over Judy. 'You *see*? He *knows* I'm here. He will have seen my car in the parking area and my case in the hall.' A flush of excitement stained her cheeks and she moved to stand near the top of the stairs, as though waiting to embrace him.

Judy remained standing beside the alcove table, her legs feeling as though they could hardly hold her. What would be Ryan's reaction to Cynthia's presence? she wondered. How would he handle this situation? And then another query hit her. Just how long had he been here? Had he heard her confess that she loved him? Her cheeks burned at the thought of it.

Even as the questions swirled in her mind Ryan reached the landing. He glanced from one to the other then drawled, 'Hi, Cynthia, what brings you here? Another investment problem?'

'Not exactly, Ryan, *darling*. I'm here because I couldn't wait any longer to be with you. Craig told me that she'd be gone by now...'

'Oh. Well, after I'd spoken to him I changed my mind. We don't leave until tomorrow. Didn't Judy tell you?' Ryan ignored the hissing gasp that escaped Cynthia and strode to where Judy stood. Taking her in his arms, he said, 'I'm sorry to have been so long in getting home, my dearest, but when I told Craig we're getting married he wanted to know all the details. I'd like him to be my best man.'

'Craig...?' Judy croaked, while making an effort to think clearly. Ryan's action had come as a shock, but she told herself he was putting on an act to give Cynthia a message. This was the way he intended handling the situation, and she'd be wise to keep her hopes under control. Nevertheless, a tremor of excitement shot through her.

Ryan grinned as he went on, 'I've got our flight tickets and the all-important *you know what*. I hope you'll like it.'

She gulped, while staring at him in a dazed manner. 'You know what?' she echoed, feeling bewildered. What on earth was he talking about?

Hugging her joyously, he said, 'Didn't I tell you I had shopping to do? It was more than just aftershave and tooth-paste.'

Cynthia had had enough. Her temper rose to the top. 'What is this?' she ranted at Ryan, her face becoming scar-let with anger.

Ryan held Judy even closer to him as he turned to look at Cynthia. 'What does it look like? Surely it's obvious?'

'But I've come to be with you,' she shrieked on a high-pitched note.

His voice hardened. 'Did I ask you to do so, Cynthia?'

'Well...no...not in actual words... But I thought... I felt sure it was what you'd want me to do. After all, you've given my affairs so much attention...I thought you were saying you wanted me to be beside you.'

'Then you were damned stupid,' Ryan gritted at her. 'Haven't you realised it was Craig who asked me to keep an eye on your affairs? Haven't I told you that you should go back to him? And there's something else you might as well know. There is only one woman I want beside me—and that woman is Judy.'

Judy gazed up at Ryan wonderingly. She could hardly believe her ears. Ryan was definitely telling Cynthia where she stood—and it wasn't beside him. Surely this was more than just an act for the sake of being rid of Cynthia? Her heart began to thump as hope soared, and, clinging to him, she raised her face for his kiss.

'A most touching scene,' Cynthia sneered. 'I'm still not convinced, Ryan, that you have any intention of...of mar-rying *her*.'

'No?' He turned to stare at Cynthia. 'Then perhaps this will help to make it look authentic.' Dipping a hand into his jacket pocket, he drew forth a small dark blue velvet-covered box. It was flicked open to reveal an oval sapphire surrounded by diamonds—an engagement ring which he slipped on to the third finger of Judy's left hand. 'I thought it would match your pendant,' he told Judy.

Judy's jaw sagged as she gazed at the ring. 'You really do mean it,' she whispered, in a barely audible tone.

'Of course I mean it,' he assured her firmly. 'Haven't I told you I never say things I don't mean? I love you, Judy, and I know you love me.' The last words were murmured against her ear, then he kissed her again, holding her closely.

The sight of their embrace was too much for Cynthia. She went berserk. 'You've stolen him from me,' she screeched at Judy in a frenzied rage, her arms flailing wildly.

It was only Ryan's quick action that prevented her from dealing Judy a blow. His arm shot out to hold her off, pushing her away from Judy, causing her to overbalance and fall to the floor, where she landed on one knee.

A cry of pain escaped her, but she picked herself up, and then examined her knee. 'You did that on purpose—you deliberately tried to hurt me,' she stormed at Ryan, her face again scarlet with fury as she flung the accusation at him.

He had no sympathy for her. 'Damned rot—you did it yourself, by attacking Judy. How *dare* you attempt to injure my future wife?' he blazed at her with sudden rage.

Cynthia took a deep breath to control her temper. 'I'm sorry…' she lied, and then, making an effort to speak quietly, she tried again. 'Ryan, dear—can't we talk?' Her tone was now pleading.

'No, we can't. You've just had your say!' Ryan gritted impatiently. 'Now then, do I have to spell it out? Judy and I have our future to plan and much to talk about. We'd be grateful if you'd take yourself off. *And don't forget your suitcase.*' His last words sounded like a low snarl.

Cynthia appeared to realise she had no option but to leave. Her green eyes glittered as they swept Judy with a look of intense hatred, then she limped towards the stairs with all the dignity she could muster. And that was the last they saw of her.

The slam of the front door echoing through the house brought a sigh of relief from Judy where she stood with her head resting against Ryan's shoulder. His arms were still about her, but the next instant she found herself being lifted and carried towards the living-room settee. As they settled themselves upon it she stared at the ring on her finger. 'I can hardly believe that this is for real,' she said in a voice filled with emotion. 'I'm afraid I'll wake up.'

'It's for real and for ever,' Ryan assured her between kisses. 'I'm sorry it had to happen the way it did. Not at all as I'd planned. I wanted moonlight and roses—romance and all the trimmings. But it was the suitcase in the hall that threw it all out of gear.'

Judy chuckled. 'You guessed?'

'I certainly did. When I arrived home I recognised Cynthia's car. I thought she'd come with a question concerning her money matters, but when I saw that her suitcase had already been carried into the house I knew she'd arrived with every intention of moving in. You were bang on correct when you said she'd ignore my friendship with Craig—and you were also right when you said she's a determined woman.'

'Poor Cynthia. I feel sorry for her,' Judy's sympathetic nature forced her to admit.

Ryan went on, 'I was staring at the suitcase, pondering over the best course to take, when I heard your voices coming from upstairs. Your own words, my darling, told me what to do.'

'They did...?' She looked at him blankly.

'When I heard you say you had faith in me, that you trusted me implicitly and that you'd follow me to the ends of the earth, I could see the course clearly. And when I heard you say you loved me, I decided to jump the gun and act as though our engagement had already become established. To be honest, I suspected that you loved me. I'd seen it in your eyes—I'd felt it in your responses.'

'I didn't know that you loved me,' Judy said, revelling in the feel of his arms encircling her body.

'It's been necessary to keep a tight rein on myself,' he explained. 'I feel as though I've known you for years and years, but I've had to keep reminding myself it's only just over a week. I haven't wanted to rush you—to sweep you off your feet. It's been difficult, but I've had to hold myself back to give you time to know your own feelings.'

'Darling Ryan—I know that I love you very much.'

'I also wanted to give you time to know me better. You can't imagine how I felt when you continued to believe the worst of me—'

'I was stupid,' she cut in hastily. 'But whatever I believed it didn't stop me from loving you. I just couldn't help myself...'

His lips found hers in a long kiss, then he said, 'Do you recall the advice I gave you about not being caught on the rebound?'

She laughed. 'You mean the warning against falling flat on my face at the feet of a handsome stranger? I remember how cross you were with me over Noel...I mean Frank.'

'Well, I knew then who'd fallen flat on his face at the feet of a beautiful girl. I was as jealous as hell. I didn't want him stepping in to upset my real plan, which was to marry you.'

She looked at him wonderingly. 'I thought your plan just concerned your holiday, which had been interrupted by Robin and myself.'

'The "holiday" is to include a honeymoon in Singapore. When we have a wedding date I'll make the reservations. You will marry me? You haven't any ideas of living together in a trial marriage? I want you as my wife.'

Judy laughed happily. 'Darling, I'm longing to be your wife.' Then she asked shyly, 'When did you first realise you loved me?'

'It was when I gave you the tapestry. I said that when you left you could take it with you—but even as I said those words I was rocked by the knowledge that I didn't want you to leave this place.'

'You kept it well hidden. I had no idea...'

'That's because I fought against it. I was a confirmed bachelor. I told myself it was a flash-in-the-pan infatuation. But each day the thought of your departure became more unbearable.' Ryan's arms tightened about her.

'You knew you needed a woman in the house?' Judy asked teasingly.

'Only if that woman could be you,' he declared firmly.

Pretending to be serious, she said, 'In that case I must hurry to get my trousseau together. My grandmother said that all brides in her day had a dozen or more of everything for the linen cupboard.'

'I suspect she was thinking of her own grandmother. There's no need for you to worry about a trousseau. We'll have a wonderful shopping spree when we reach Singapore.'

Judy's heart was so full of joy she could only gaze at him adoringly. There was no longer any need to keep her love for him hidden. She could now pour it all over him with complete abandon.

He said, 'Would you like to go out to dinner this evening?'

She was horrified by the thought. 'Oh, no...no. These moments are too precious to be spent in a restaurant.'

'I was only joking.' He grinned. 'This evening I've no intention of going further than the bedroom. Later we'll find a snack in the fridge, if we happen to be hungry.'

'Later...?' Judy caught her breath as his meaning dawned upon her. Suddenly it was difficult to look at him, and she hid her face against his neck.

Sensing her shyness, he said, 'You'll be wearing this gold outfit on the plane tomorrow?'

'No. I was just about to take it off when Cynthia arrived.'

'Go and do so now, my darling,' he murmured in her ear. 'I'll bolt the doors before Kate's curiosity brings her up the back stairs.'

'Kate? Why would she come at this hour?'

'Ostensibly to borrow teabags or a cup of sugar. In reality to learn why Cynthia left in a rage. Her kitchen overlooks our parking area, and Kate doesn't miss much. I'll bet she witnessed the saga of the suitcase—its arrival and departure.'

Judy shook her head. In defence of Kate she said, 'I told her you'll be coming to Christchurch with me, and that you'll be staying in my parents' home. She'll guess that *that* would make Cynthia irate.'

'Nevertheless, I'll bolt the doors now,' Ryan declared with quiet determination. 'I'll not tolerate intrusion tonight of all nights...' He left the settee and went downstairs to check the front door.

His last words sent quivers of breathless anticipation through Judy. Was it only a short time ago that she'd been feeling so overwrought? Now she was floating on air. Instinctively, she knew that tonight she'd be giving herself to Ryan. And she knew that from now onwards they'd belong to each other. Like the gannets, they'd be mated for life.

Her legs felt as though they'd barely carry her as she made her way to her bedroom, where she pulled the gold woollen top over her head and stepped out of her skirt. And, despite the deep breaths she took to steady her nerves, her hands shook as she folded them. Clad only in her bra, panties, tights and shoes, she was placing the suit in her suitcase when Ryan stepped into the room.

He was now wearing a green towelling wrap that came down to his bare knees, the top being sufficiently open to reveal the crisp dark hairs on his broad chest. For a moment he stood still, to stare at Judy in her half-dressed state, then he strode forward to swing her up into his arms. 'Kick your shoes off, my darling,' he muttered in a low, deep voice. 'You'll not be wearing them in bed—nor anything else.'

There were two light thuds as the shoes landed on the floor, then Judy clung to him as he carried her towards his bedroom. She noticed that the lights had been left off and the curtains undrawn, and as he laid her gently on the wide bed she found herself again bathed by the glowing magic of golden beams coming through the window from the street lamps. It was all so lovely it seemed unreal.

But there was nothing unreal in the way Ryan disposed of every barrier between them, and within moments her few remaining garments were tossed out on to the floor. For several long moments she lay tense and inwardly trembling, while becoming conscious of the maleness of the naked body lying beside her.

'Relax, my beloved—just relax...' Ryan's words were murmured huskily against her lips.

His deep voice had a soothing effect, and with her nerves calmed her desire suddenly became free to match his own. Clasped within the haven of his arms, her body caught fire beneath the magic touch of hands that lifted her gently towards the heights. And as she pulsated with delicious sensations she became filled with a passionate yearning to give and give until it hurt.

She also knew that this was only the beginning of life in the hermit's cave. Ahead of them lay years of loving and giving to each other. Ryan was her mate, and the future looked as golden as the beams that turned the bedroom into an enchanted place. Silently, she made a vow to keep it that way.

MILLS & BOON®

Nearly

Weds!

From your favourite romance authors:

Betty Neels
Making Sure of Sarah

Carole Mortimer
The Man She'll Marry

Penny Jordan
They're Wed Again!

Enjoy an eventful trip to the altar with
three new wedding stories—when
nearly weds become *newly weds!*

Available from 19th March 1999

MILLS & BOON®

Makes any time special™

*Bestselling themed romances brought
back to you by popular demand*

Each month By Request brings you three
full-length novels in one beautiful volume
featuring the best of the best.

So if you missed a favourite Romance
the first time around, here is your chance
to relive the magic from some of our
most popular authors.

Look out for
Sole Paternity in March 1999
**featuring Miranda Lee, Robyn Donald
and Sandra Marton**

FREE

4 BOOKS
AND A SURPRISE GIFT!

We would like to take this opportunity to thank you for reading this Mills & Boon® book by offering you the chance to take FOUR more specially selected titles from the Enchanted™ series absolutely FREE! We're also making this offer to introduce you to the benefits of the Reader Service™—

★ FREE home delivery
★ FREE monthly Newsletter
★ FREE gifts and competitions
★ Exclusive Reader Service discounts
★ Books available before they're in the shops

Accepting these FREE books and gift places you under no obligation to buy; you may cancel at any time, even after receiving your free shipment. Simply complete your details below and return the entire page to the address below. *You don't even need a stamp!*

YES! Please send me 4 free Enchanted books and a surprise gift. I understand that unless you hear from me, I will receive 6 superb new titles every month for just £2.40 each, postage and packing free. I am under no obligation to purchase any books and may cancel my subscription at any time. The free books and gift will be mine to keep in any case.

N9EC

Ms/Mrs/Miss/Mr ....Initials....................................
BLOCK CAPITALS PLEASE

Surname...

Address..

....

....Postcode ....

Send this whole page to:
THE READER SERVICE, FREEPOST CN81, CROYDON, CR9 3WZ
(Eire readers please send coupon to: P.O. Box 4546, DUBLIN 24.)

Offer valid in UK and Eire only and not available to current Reader Service subscribers to this series. We reserve the right to refuse an application and applicants must be aged 18 years or over. Only one application per household. Terms and prices subject to change without notice. Offer expires 30th September 1999. As a result of this application, you may receive further offers from Harlequin Mills & Boon and other carefully selected companies. If you would prefer not to share in this opportunity please write to The Data Manager at the address above.

Mills & Boon is a registered trademark owned by Harlequin Mills & Boon Limited.
Enchanted is being used as a trademark.

MILLS & BOON®

Makes any time special™

The Regency Collection

Mills & Boon® is delighted to bring back, for a limited period, 12 of our favourite Regency Romances for you to enjoy.

These special books will be available for you to collect each month from May, and with two full-length Historical Romance™ novels in each volume they are great value at only £4.99.

Volume One available from 7th May